THE DIRE BEAR CAFE

THE DIRE BEAR CAFE

CHINLE MILLER

Yellow Cat
PUBLISHING

Cover by Cary Cox

A special thank you to Geerling Engineering for the hot dog as a receiver idea.

For Mike and Joan Venator

CONTENTS

1

Emery County Sheriff Bud Shumway sat in the back booth of his wife's Melon Rind Cafe, his well-worn brown Stetson drifting down over his eyebrows as he tilted his head, listening.

Was that really the sound of a train whistle? Trains in his little town of Green River, Utah weren't unusual, but being able to hear one while inside the cafe was. It then dawned on him that things were extraordinarily quiet because he was the only customer, though his wife, Wilma Jean, and her helper, Maureen, were in the cafe's kitchen.

Pushing his hat back up, Bud wondered if maybe the reason the cafe was so empty was because there was something going on in town that he wasn't aware of, maybe some shenanigans conjured up by Maureen's husband, Mayor Howie McPherson, though he couldn't recall him mentioning anything. Green River's biggest event, Melon Days, wouldn't happen for a few weeks.

Maybe he should get back down to his office, though he'd forwarded the phone there to his cell phone, which everyone in town knew to call anyway if they needed anything. Besides, nothing much ever happened in Green River, which was fine by him, as it meant he could occasionally slip away to enjoy a cup of coffee and maybe even a piece of blueberry pie, assuming there was any left from the break-fast crowd.

Train long gone, his gaze now went to the half-dozen pictures gracing the cafe walls—a big silver Amtrak engine coming down the tracks, colorful desert flowers, and the petroglyphs in nearby Tusher Canyon.

The photos were printed on metal, which made them pop, and Bud thought they looked much more impressive hanging on the cafe walls than they had on his computer screen. He'd had them made at a print shop in the nearby town of Price, where he and Wilma Jean now owned a house, the result of one of her many business deals.

Bud was thinking that even though he was maybe starting to get half-good as a photographer, it was still somewhat embarrassing to see his photos hanging on the cafe walls, especially with price tags. It would probably be better if his wife didn't own the cafe, for he preferred that people thought the photos were there on their own merit.

Oh well, such were the ways of the business world, he mused, sipping his coffee. Maybe someday someone would actually buy one. He wondered if that would make him a professional photographer—or did being a professional mean the majority of one's income came from photography? Or maybe it simply referred to the level of one's skills.

Whatever it meant, he was pretty sure he didn't qualify, as much as he enjoyed taking photos, and he probably should ask his wife to take them down. After all, he'd had them printed to put on the walls of their newly acquired house, not in the cafe.

Just then, two men walked in, pausing to look around. One was fairly young, maybe in his early thirties, while Bud figured the other could easily be the fellow's grandfather, gray-haired and slightly stooped, yet having that air of dignity that comes from years of experience and knowledge.

The younger one had long dark hair pulled back in a pony tail, and Bud thought they must be natives, or was he supposed to say indigenous or even First Nations? He knew a couple of natives, and they called themselves Indians, so he found it all rather confusing, preferring to just call them people.

He wondered where they were from—the nearest reservation was owned by the Utes and was several hours north near the town of Vernal, though he knew some of the native people didn't live on reservations any more.

The younger man was dressed in a yellow t-shirt, jeans, and sneakers, and the older man also wore jeans, but with an old-style Western red plaid shirt, cowboy boots, and a Stetson hat similar to Bud's, though much more worn and tattered. The contrast of a beautiful beaded hatband made the hat look even more ragged, and the fellow's large silver belt buckle added to the old-school air.

They nodded hello, the younger one studying the sheriff's insignia on Bud's shirt for a moment. Sitting in a nearby booth, the young guy opened a menu while the old man studied one of Bud's photos above them of the Tusher Canyon petroglyphs.

Looking up, the young man said, "Look, Gramps, it says you can get breakfast any time, and they have biscuits and gravy, your favorite."

Just then, having heard the cafe door open and close, Maureen appeared from the back, carrying two cups and a carafe of coffee, looking at them questioningly.

The two men nodded their heads, and she poured them each a cup, making sure the small bowl on the table that held little tubs of half-and-half was full, as well as the one holding sugar cubes. She then told them she'd be back for their order, refilled Bud's cup, and was gone.

Noting that his grandfather was still studying the photo above them, the young man said, "Gramps, forget the picture and figure out what you want to eat. We don't have a lot of time."

Ignoring him, the grandfather asked Bud, "Do you know who took this?"

Bud, now feeling a little embarrassed and wishing he'd gone back to his office, replied, "I did, and if you're interested, I think the price might be negotiable. My wife thinks these are worth more than they probably actually are."

The young man replied, "No, it's a nice photo. It's probably worth even more. You're the sheriff here?"

"Where is this?" the old man asked. Bud was now beginning to detect a slight accent, one he thought he recognized. "It's in a canyon not too far from here," he replied.

The old man added, "Can you tell us how to get there?"

"Sure," Bud replied. "I'll draw you a map. It's not far, but you need high clearance. Say, are you fellows Canadian by any chance?"

A slight moment of what Bud thought looked like panic crossed the young man's face, who replied, "I'm American, from Salt Lake, but my grandfather's from Saskatchewan—a small town called Swift Current."

Bud, now drawing the route to Tusher Canyon on a napkin, replied distractedly, "There's a Swift Current up in Glacier National Park. It may just be a common place name, but maybe it was named after your town. We spent our vacation up there not too long ago."

The young man, seeming to relax, said, "That's cool." He then added, "Gramps, you can just starve, since you don't seem interested in the menu. We're still a good ways from Delta. I guess you can just wait and eat when we get there, though it may be awhile."

"Don't disrespect the Grandfathers, Christian," the old man said sternly. "Remember Wanuskewin. If they want us to visit them, we'll visit them."

Just then, Maureen returned, and Bud stood to leave, handing the old man the napkin with the map he'd drawn, wondering why he would refer to the rock art as the Grandfathers—or was he referring to himself somehow? And why were they headed for Delta, a small agricultural town out on the edge of Basin and Range country, almost in Nevada? There was nothing there that would attract tourists, though maybe they were going to see family. And why were they interested in Tusher Canyon?

As he walked out the door, Bud heard the young man named Christian, say, "Two orders of biscuits and gravy, please."

Walking to his sheriff's Land Cruiser, Bud noted a white Chevy Silverado crew cab parked in front of the cafe and figured it belonged to the pair inside. He could tell it wasn't a four-wheel drive, and he figured they might have trouble in the canyon. Maybe he'd drive out there later and make sure they weren't stuck.

As he walked by their vehicle, he noted it had a sturdy-looking magnetic antenna attached to the roof, and he then caught a glimpse of something blue through the partially opened back window, something that looked like a pile of dyed feathers.

Just then, several locals entered the cafe, and Bud nodded to them, glad to see the lull was temporary. Hearing another train whistle, he decided to go down to the station and watch the train come in. Maybe he would take a few photos, though he swore he wouldn't get any printed this time, no matter what his wife said.

As he backed into the street, he thought again of the pair in the cafe, wondering what had brought the grandfather all the way from Canada.

Little did he suspect that he would soon be knee-deep in a mystery featuring them, a mystery set in a place even more mysterious and poignant feeling than the distant whistles of his beloved trains—a lonely land of long views and blue distances, a land of the now-extinct dire bear, a land known as the Wasatch Plateau, Ute for *low place in high mountains.*

2

It was later that day, and Bud sat in his office, reading the latest issue of *Outdoor Photography*, Mayor Howie across from him with his long legs propped on a nearby chair as he wrote something in a small notebook.

Looking up, Bud asked, "Are you opening the drive-in soon? I could sure use one of your barbecue sandwiches."

Putting his feet down, Howie replied, "Shoots, I need to get over there. This little project I'm working on got me all sidetracked, and I kind of let time get away from me. Come on over in a half-hour and I'll make you a sandwich."

"Exactly what project are you working on, Howie? Something for Melon Days?"

"I wish," Howie replied. "I still have lots to do on that. But Sheriff, I have to answer your question by first giving some background, or else my little project's going to seem kind of weird."

Putting the notebook and pen in his pocket, Howie continued. "See, I had kind of a rough night. When we first bought the house, Maureen was all into decorating things, and she had me install a small shelf up above our bed where she put some knickknacks she liked—some old purple bottles with dried flowers in them. By the way, did you know that knickknack is one of the only words in English with the k and n sounds together?"

"No kidding? I always thought the k was silent." Bud replied somewhat absent-mindedly, wanting to get back to the article he'd been reading about how to photograph fireflies, though he knew his odds of ever seeing one in his little desert town were slim.

"Anyway," Howie continued, standing to go. "Last night, I was sound asleep when our Maine coon cat Bodie was catting around and decided he wanted to jump up on that shelf. What got into him I'll never know, as he's had lots of time to try it out, but he picked the middle of the night, and of course, it all came right down—down onto my head where I'd been sound asleep. Let me ask you, Sheriff, if that happened to you, would you quietly wake up and gently pet the cat and then go back to sleep?"

"Probably not," Bud replied, trying hard not to laugh.

"Well, I don't know any human who would, and I sure didn't."

"Didn't what?" Bud asked, closing the magazine.

"Didn't go quietly into that good night, to quote some poem I read in high school," Howie replied. "No sir, I emerged from a nice quiet dream into a world of chaos, and I let rip a few choice words that I don't think my wife's ever heard me use. I mean, Sheriff, I'd just been knocked on the head by some old bottles, and a cat was sprawled out on my face, so what would anyone expect? And of course it woke up little Malcolm, who's been sleeping with us lately, as he's at that stage where he thinks there's a monster under his bed. So I not only got whacked in the head with a bunch of old bottles, dried flowers, and a big fat hairy cat, but I also got chewed out by Maureen for cussing around Malcolm."

"Well, that certainly doesn't seem fair," Bud said. "But Howie, what does all that have to do with this project you're working on?"

"Well, Sheriff, I'm making a list of words you can use when you're irritated, words that won't offend anyone—you know, words that are 'grandma approved.' I'm going to memorize and field test them so next time I don't get my head bit off."

"Why not just leave the shelf down?" Bud asked. "But what's on your list so far?"

"So far, I've got *dad blame it, dad gummit, dad blast it, son of a biscuit, son of a biscuit eater, son of a Baptist preacher, son of a nutcracker,* and *son of a rabid ferret.*"

"Son of a rabid ferret?" Bud laughed.

"Write down any you think of, Bud," Howie said, heading out the door. "But you need to answer your phone. See you later, Sheriff."

Watching Howie cross the street to his drive-in, Bud picked up his phone.

"Sheriff's Office. Bud speaking."

"Is this Bud?" a raspy voice asked.

"It is," Bud replied.

"Bud, this is Gord Marsing—you know, the guy who has the place out on Hastings. I was just up Tusher Canyon and saw something you should know about."

"That's funny, Gordon. I was thinking about going out there as soon as I had lunch. What's going on?"

"Well, I was driving up the canyon real slow, looking for a steer that got out of the pasture this morning. I got up to that one big petroglyph panel and was turning around when I saw a white Silverado parked there. I thought maybe they were stuck, 'cause there was a fellow up in the rocks waving something around, like maybe he was trying to find a cell phone signal. Had to be half goat to even get up there. There was an old guy by the road taking pictures of the panel. Nothing unusual about that, but the guy up on the cliffs seemed weird."

Gord paused until Bud thought the connection may have dropped, then finally continued.

"I was going to ask if they needed help, but before I could say *duck and roll*, another pickup, a green one, comes barreling down the road, dust everywhere, and it roared right up to the Silverado. The fellow up on the cliffs must've seen it coming, because by then he was back down, and he and the old guy jumped into their truck and took off. It's a wonder I didn't get runned over."

"Was it anyone local?"

"No, never seen the green pickup before, and nobody around here has a white Silverado. But there was too much dust to make out a whole lot, and there was a white SUV following the pickup, also driving like a bat out of hell. I just want to know what this country's coming to when a man can't even take a half-abandoned back road without almost getting himself runned over. Green River's getting bad enough with all these tourists coming in to buy melons—no offense, Sheriff, as I know you grow 'em—and next thing you know, they'll be puttin' in a traffic light."

"Out in Tusher Canyon?" Bud kidded. "Did you find the steer?"

"You know what I mean, and yes, I did find the steer. It was over by the barn when I got back. Hadn't even gone anywhere. I just didn't look good enough. Good thing, too, or it would've got runned over."

"OK, Gord. Thanks for letting me know."

"I ain't done, Bud. As the Silverado took off, the guys in the SUV yelled at the guys in it as they went by, then they stopped and asked me if I knew where they were going. I asked them what was going on and they said they were fox hunting, then they also took off. Sheriff, I can't imagine going out on a fox hunt in this country, 'cause your odds of finding one are slim, especially if you're juoksentelisinkohan. It just seemed strange."

Bud asked, "Could you repeat that, Gord?"

"I said, I've only seen a few fox around here, and those were down by the river."

"No, no," Bud replied. "That long word you used, that yoke-sen thing."

Gord laughed. "My grandparents came from Finland and used that word a lot, especially to describe me when I was a kid."

"Say it again, Gord, real slow. What does it mean?"

"Juoksentelisinkohan. YOKE-sen-TELL-ee-seen-ko-hahn," Gord replied. It's Finnish for *I wonder if I should wander around aimlessly.* The word means you're thinking about it, though these fellows looked like they were actually doing it."

"I need to remember that one," Bud said. "But the Fins sit around wondering if they should wander around aimlessly? Sounds like my kind of place, especially if they have a word for it, and Finland's generally considered to be the world's happiest country. But did you see any guns or hear any shooting?"

"No."

"Can you describe exactly where all this happened?"

"Right at that big panel up in the rocks with what looks like a big necklace under some bighorn. You know the one, it's the biggest panel out there, about midway up the canyon."

"OK," Bud replied. "If you see any of those vehicles around, give me a call. I'm going to go out there as soon as I have lunch."

Gord asked, "You goin' over to Howie's? I'll meet you there. My wife's given me marching orders to get some garden stuff on sale at the hardware store, so I might as well go shopping on a full stomach. I've heard that's the way to do it so you don't go buying stuff you don't need just because it looks good."

"At a hardware store?" Bud asked.

"They sell candy bars, Bud, Snickers and Milky Ways."

"I guess that *could* get dangerous on an empty stomach," Bud laughed. "Anyway, I'll see you at the drive-in."

He hung up, wondering if the Silverado Gordon had seen was the same one that had been parked in front of the cafe. He had no idea why anyone would be fox hunting in Tusher Canyon, but he'd go out after lunch and see if he could find anything unusual, though he figured it was just another of the many odd behaviors he knew were associated with the human race, though usually nothing much came of anything.

As he walked across the street to Howie's, the anticipation of a good barbecue sandwich pushed out all other thoughts, except that of maybe going by the hardware store after lunch to get a couple of candy bars.

After that, he'd run by the bungalow and get the dogs and a thermos of coffee, then head on up Tusher Canyon, where maybe he'd sit on a big rock and wonder if he should wander around aimlessly.

3

Bud drove up the dirt road that led to Tusher Canyon, the dogs' noses sniffing whatever was the scent du jour, which he figured must be rabbitbrush, as it was autumn and the thick yellow blooms dusted the edges of the narrow two-track.

They were in Bud's old tan Toyota FJ, as he preferred it to the sheriff's Land Cruiser when he had the dogs. Lindie, his Carolina dingo, rode on the front seat, her head hanging out the window, and Pierre and Hoppie, a dachshund and Basset hound, rode in the back, barely able to stick their little noses out, both being short.

The drive would make a nice afternoon outing, Bud thought, even though the canyon was technically not in Emery County, as the county line went up the middle of the river. He and his friend Hum Stocks, Sheriff of Radium County, had a mutual agreement for him to patrol areas close to Green River, so this technically counted as being on the job. Even though Bud had plenty of territory to cover with his own county's 4,452 square miles, there typically wasn't much going on in its redrock canyons, alpine meadows, and desert wilderness.

As the road entered the canyon proper, Bud had one last view of the gray buttes of the Bookcliffs framing the north edge of town, which included the 5,247-foot Gunnison Butte, named for the early explorer, and the 5,767-foot Battleship Butte, which looked a good deal like its namesake.

Thinking back on his metal photos in the cafe, he recalled seeing a photo of Gunnison Butte by the early photographer William Henry Jackson that had been taken sometime in the 1880s and developed using the albumen silver print technique.

Being interested in photography, he'd looked the process up and found that it was the original technique for printing on paper, using a glossy coating of egg whites. Prior to that, photos had been printed on metal.

The thought reminded him of Howie and one of his favorite sayings, "The more things change, the more they remain the same." It seemed true that the fundamental nature of things never did change, even though superficial changes might make one think otherwise. It seemed ironic that photos had gone from being developed on metal to paper and back again to metal.

Whatever changes one might see in their short lifetime, Bud felt that the nearby Bookcliffs, called the *Books* by the locals, would always be there, unchanging in their desert magnificence, even though his geologist friend Shorty had told him that there was evidence that the cliffs once extended to the opposite side of I-70 and had eroded miles back, and not even that long ago in geologic time.

He'd read somewhere that the Books were the longest continuous escarpment in the world, beginning east near Grand Junction, Colorado, and running west all the way to Price, Utah, a distance of over 250 miles, where they then merged into what was called the Wasatch Plateau. Shorty had also told him the cliffs got their name because of Cretaceous sandstone that capped the buttes, making them look like bookshelves.

Above the high walls of the Books were the tall blue-stem grasses and aspen forests of the Roan and Tavaputs plateaus, the stair-stepping cliffs below them acting as natural barriers, making sure that vast areas of the region remained unexplored, with many undocumented petroglyphs and pit houses, remnants of the ancient Fremont and Barrier or Archaic peoples.

Tusher Canyon cut through the Books, and if one took the left-hand branch, they could access the first tier of cliffs where the canyon transitioned from desert to higher elevations. Like nearby thoroughfares such as Coal and Horse canyons, Tusher was a way for the ancient people to move with the seasons from higher to lower elevations and vice versa.

The road split, and Bud took the main branch, knowing the large panel Gord had mentioned was in that part of the canyon.

Soon, he stood beneath a large rock art panel, a hodgepodge of images of deer with huge antlers, bighorn sheep, bear-claw necklaces, assorted lines of dots, and what looked like a large bull, though he knew there were no cattle in the Americas until the time of Columbus.

He'd seen many such petroglyphs and pictographs, the difference in the terms being whether or not the images were pecked into the rock (petroglyphs) or painted with vegetative and mineral dyes (pictographs). The slabs and faces of Utah's many canyons created the perfect canvas for ancient people to tell their stories, and Bud suspected that some of the art also depicted maps telling others the lay of the land.

He knew that a certain style had been dated to around 5,000 years ago and was all that was left of the Barrier or Archaic people. He'd also seen art that depicted riders on horses, which was more recent, made by the Utes, who acquired horses from neighboring tribes in the 1500s.

Anyone who'd been in the canyon country long soon acquired the skill of spotting good places for rock art, as it was almost always on the protected faces of large rocks or cliffs, many bearing desert varnish, a blackish manganese-iron deposit that gradually formed on exposed cliff faces. Older art gradually got darker as new varnish slowly covered it, making for some interesting contrasts.

Standing in front of the panel, Bud studied the rocks above, wondering how Christian had managed to climb them, though he thought he saw a possible route up. It looked too tenuous for him, so he began searching below the panel, wondering if he weren't on a bit of a fox hunt himself, the fox in this case being Gord's imagination. Nothing he'd reported had been illegal, and there were no signs of foul play—or of any kind of play, for that matter.

Having looked around, Bud decided there was nothing of any interest to be found, so he let the dogs out of the FJ so they could sniff around. He would kick back on a large nearby rock while they pretended they were hunting rabbits, enjoying the early autumn sun.

He loved being in the canyons this time of year, for the skies seemed bluer than usual, the desert heat had mellowed, and the foliage that lined the seasonal waterways was beginning to turn brilliant reds and golds, announcing that everything would soon be nodding off for the winter.

Leaning back against the cliff face, he watched the dogs sniff around as he tried not to drift off, the barbecue sandwich from Howie's Drive-In finally taking hold and making him sleepy.

He needed to get his thermos of coffee from the FJ, he decided, slumping down a bit more. Just then, something sharp poked his back and he involuntarily yelled out and jumped up, wide-awake, thinking he'd maybe been stung by a scorpion.

The dogs were soon there, tails wagging, wondering what was going on, as Bud cautiously looked all around the rock he'd been sitting on. It was then that he saw something shiny and metallic poking out from a crack in the rock right where he'd been leaning.

It was some kind of wire, long and thin with a small ball on the end. Grabbing the ball part, he gently pulled, and out from the crack appeared a small plastic bag, the wire sticking from where the bag's opening had been tied closed.

Carefully opening the bag, he found it contained a small box-like object with a pair of knit mittens wrapped around it, probably for protection, he figured. Pulling it out, he could see it was a small radio with an antenna! It had been there the entire time, and he would've never noticed it if he hadn't managed to lean against it.

He removed the mittens, and the radio fit perfectly into the palm of his hand. After brushing off the dirt, he could read the word *Yaesu* beneath a small screen, with a bank of small buttons underneath that. The antenna was a good two feet long, and the rig had the solid feel of a somewhat expensive device. In fact, it reminded him of his sheriff's Motorola handheld radio, though smaller and with more buttons.

He now examined the mittens, which were made of a dark-purple yarn with what looked like a yellow lightning-bolt pattern going across the middle of each hand and wrapping around the back. The yarn was soft and felt like fine wool, and he noted that whoever had done the knitting had done a beautiful job on all but the lightning bolts, which were rough and full of tiny knots that looked like small mistakes, though they weren't that noticeable unless you rubbed your hand across them.

He put the radio and mittens on the passenger seat, then gathered the dogs back into the FJ and was soon on his way back to Green River, wondering who had left a walkie-talkie and pair of mittens out in the canyon, though he suspected it had something to do with Christian and the escapade Gord had called him about.

As he emerged from the canyon, the radio crackled with static, and a voice said, "QRZ AFØXN. This is KFØSTL."

A second voice responded, "KFØSTL. We're meeting at the henhouse. AFØXN, tally ho, and over."

"Roger that. See you there, Earl. KFØSTL."

The radio was again silent, and Bud headed back to town. He'd drop the dogs off, then go back to his office, but only after cruising around a bit to see if he could spot the Silverado. Maybe he could get their radio back to them.

As he turned onto Hastings, a brown pickup with a white topper covered in dust slowed and turned onto the road into the canyon. As it passed, he caught a glimpse of its plates, which read, *Saskatchewan, Land of Living Skies*. For a moment, he thought maybe it was the pickup Gord had described as following the Silverado, but he then remembered Gord had said that one was green.

He found it curious to see more Canadians, but Green River saw visitors from all over, so he wasn't really surprised. He suspected it was all just tourists having fun, hoping he wouldn't find out otherwise.

He continued on back to town, the pickup going its way on up the canyon.

4

Bud sat under a big cottonwood whose leaves were beginning to show a hint of gold, the dogs rolling around in the dirt after dipping in the shallow muddy water of a nearby irrigation ditch as he played *Red River Valley* on his harmonica.

He figured they must wonder where all the water had gone, as normally they would be able to swim and chase sticks in the flow, but the ditches had been shut down by his farm manager, Kale, in preparation for the melon harvest. The fields were bursting with melons, and Bud knew that soon the farm would be filled with activity.

The harvest was a labor-intensive affair with hired pickers who tested each melon for ripeness by thumping on it before cutting it from the vine, as watermelons were too fragile to be harvested with machines. The melons would then be tossed along a chain of workers and stacked by the roadside, where they would be loaded into trucks, making their way to grocery stores and distributors all across the country, with a few held back for Melon Days and the farm's roadside stand.

The reject melons and broken vines would then be plowed under, the end of another growing season, which had begun in the spring, when each melon was planted by hand. Growing melons was a labor of love and hard work, but fortunately, Kale managed it all, freeing Bud to do his sheriff's duties and other important things, like practicing his harmonica, though fiddling with it might be a better way to describe things.

Throwing Lindie a stick, Bud savored the peace and quiet, knowing that he'd want to avoid the farm through the harvest. He'd decided to bring the dogs out before dropping them off at the bungalow and heading back to his office—it was a good excuse to disengage from everything and kick back for a half-hour or so.

He hadn't slept well the previous night, and he suspected it was from the incoming low-pressure system that his manager Kale had mentioned, possibly what had also made Howie's cat Bodie restless.

He'd driven around town looking for the Silverado, but to no avail, and he was now wondering if he would ever be able to get the radio back to its owner, assuming it was indeed Christian's. He suspected that what Gord had witnessed was Christian up in the rocks waving the radio around, trying to get a signal, though for what purpose Bud had no idea, as they could've just driven back out of the canyon where reception would be better. And why had he ditched the radio?

Walking into the nearest field, dogs at his heels, he picked up a small round melon, pulling it from the vine. Sitting back under the tree, he took out his pocket knife and cut into its heart. That particular field had been planted with seedless Black Diamond melons, named for their dark green color that almost looked black when in the field.

After enjoying a slice of the ruby-red fruit, he gave each of the dogs a small piece, though Lindie was the only one interested, mouthing it for a moment, then spitting it out. He was reminded of a quote from Mark Twain: "When one has tasted watermelon, he knows what angels eat." Apparently dogs and angels had different tastes, he mused.

It had been a good year for melons, Bud thought, wondering if the weather would hold for the harvest. The big front sitting over the

Pacific Northwest that Kale had mentioned looked to be headed their way, bringing lots of rain.

Green River melons were famous, the hot days and cool nights making for perfect conditions for the sugars to set, but he knew the melon business could be fickle. A number of growers had abandoned melons and switched to other crops through the years, crops such as hay and corn, which were more forgiving.

Just last year he'd lost part of a 30-acre field of Crenshaws, as some of the melons had inexplicably rotted. Fortunately, Kale had managed to sell the rest of the field to a brewer in Colorado who wanted the melons for their signature ale. It was the only reason the farm didn't lose money that year, as the brewer had been willing to pay top dollar.

The Crenshaw was one of over 1,200 varieties in the watermelon family, all of them fickle. Bud wondered how long before he and Kale would make the decision to leave the business and grow hay or corn instead of their usual crops of cantaloupe, honeydew, and melons. The problem was that nothing paid as well as melons, and Bud and Wilma Jean still owed quite a bit on the farm.

Now full of watermelon, he leaned back against the gnarled trunk of the old tree and was almost asleep when his phone rang, making him jump. He reached into his jacket pocket and answered, "Yell-ow."

"Is this Bud?" a voice asked, one he recognized as Gordon Marsing's. They'd had a pleasant enough lunch at Howie's, talking mostly about farming and such, so he was surprised to hear from him again.

"It is," he replied. "What's up, Gord?"

"Well, Bud, you told me to call if I saw any of the vehicles from up Tusher, and I just saw one, so I'm calling you, sheriff's orders."

Bud laughed. "It wasn't exactly an order, Gord, but where are they?"

"That SUV is parked in front of Howie's Drive-In, though the Silverado's not there. At least that's where they were as of about two minutes ago. If you'd been in your office, you would've seen them, and I wouldn't be doing your job for you."

"What exactly are you doing again, Gord?" Bud asked patiently, though a bit irritated. Gord had no idea where he was or what he was doing, though maybe that was a good thing.

"I'm hunting down fox hunters, Sheriff," Gord replied.

"Well, OK then, good job," Bud said, adding, "Thanks for calling."

He hung up, then loaded the dogs into the FJ after trying to brush the mud from their paws. He'd take them to the bungalow, then head to Howie's Drive-In, where he could hopefully find out who the Yaesu belonged to.

He wondered again what the guys on the radio had meant by going to the henhouse. Maybe he should ask them about this so-called fox-hunting expedition, then contact the Utah Division of Wildlife Resources.

He sighed, pulling into the bungalow's drive, sensing that his quiet reprieve before harvest was ending, but too sleepy to really think about it much.

5

"Sheriff, this is a ham radio," Howie said. "Hams call them *handy-talkies,* or *hats,* for *HT* or *handheld transceivers.* They can both transmit and receive, though they generally can't go very far. This one is made by the Japanese company Yaesu, one of the top brands, and it wasn't cheap, I can guarantee that. You need a license to operate these things."

Bud sat in a booth in Howie's Drive-In, the radio and mittens on the table. The vehicle Gord had called about was long gone, and when asked, Howie said they'd come during a rush, and he hadn't noticed anyone who seemed out of the ordinary.

Bud replied, "Ham, as in amateur radio? And why do you know so much about it?"

"Yup," Howie replied. "Amateur radio, though the amateur part just means it's not commercial. There's really nothing amateur about it, as it's a very technical hobby. Some would say kind of geeky, actually, but to be nice I'll say eggheady. My uncle was a ham, and I got my license when I was in high school, but I let it expire. My call sign was *WØRQC,* and it was still available, so I got it back."

"That's impressive, Howie. Was it hard to get?"

"Kind of. You had to pass a written test and also show you knew enough Morse code to send and receive at something like 5 or 10 words per minute—I don't remember how many exactly. But see this whip antenna? Someone added it on. It's longer and gets better reception than the original rubber duck."

"Interesting. What does QRZ mean?"

"It's what you say when you're looking for a specific person to answer. It shows you're not wanting to ragchew with just anyone. Where did you hear that?"

"When I was coming out of the canyon, the radio came on and someone said QRZ and a callsign. It makes sense now. But you know Morse code?"

"I used to," Howie replied, then added somewhat wistfully, "I should've kept it up. It's a neat hobby, but I gave it up and got caught up in other stuff."

"Like astronomy?"

"Yeah, and music—and making a living."

"And learning cuss words," Bud grinned. "How's that project going, by the way?"

"Dagnabbit, it's going good," Howie grinned, pulling the small notebook from his pocket. "I've added *jeepers*, *dang darnit*, *good gravy*, *great googly moogly*, *jeez Louise*, *great Caesar's ghost*, *mother Francis*, and *shut the front door*."

"Shut the front door?"

"Yeah, that's one that Old Man Green uses all the time. But Bud, none of them really do the job, if you know what I mean. They're not very satisfying. Have you come up with any?"

"Hows about *h-e-double-hockey-sticks* and *mother-of-pearl*?"

"Those are good ones," Howie replied, writing them down.

"What would a henhouse be?" Bud asked. "Is that special ham talk for something?"

"Nah, that's just an old trucker's expression for a greasy-spoon cafe where you can get breakfast."

"Hams and eggs, eh?" Bud replied, not wanting to tell Howie the ham guys had showed up at his drive-in after saying they were going to the henhouse.

Just then, the radio crackled.

"Someone just kerchunked the repeater, Sheriff. That's when you key it up for a short time but don't identify yourself, something you're not supposed to do. It causes the squelch detector in the repeater to activate for a few seconds. Hear that Morse code? That's the repeater identifying itself."

"Any idea where the nearest one is, Howie?" Bud asked.

"Not sure," Howie replied. "Though I know there's one up by Sunnyside on Bruin Point and one on Cedar Mountain. I'm pretty sure there's a grid out here of repeater relays. They're always up on mountains or high towers so you can communicate over obstacles, like hills and buildings, otherwise, you'd only be reaching a few miles with your handheld. But that radio's gonna run out of juice if you don't turn it off. You need a charger."

"I know," Bud replied. "I was hoping someone would come on the air so I could figure out who it belonged to."

"How could its owner use it when you've got it?" Howie asked. "You might hear other people talking, but not the owner, unless he's got another radio. I can put up a sign here in the drive-in, and maybe whoever lost it will come in."

"That's a good idea," Bud said. "I'll leave it here with you."

Howie turned off the radio, then opened the battery cover, saying, "Sheriff, it's got a bank of AA batteries all tied together. I can make up another bank, then we can listen in without worrying about it. I'll make up a couple."

"I knew you were good with telescopes and such, Howie, but I had no idea you knew electronics."

Howie guffawed. "You need to know electronics to make a battery bank? It's not like I wired a house or anything, Sheriff, though I am starting to get into old tube amps for my guitar. There's something about the sound that's really nice."

"None of that solid state stuff, eh?" Bud asked. "When are you guys playing again?"

"Well, Bud, you know that when I ran for mayor, I promised my constituency a concert by Howie and the Ramblin' Road Rangers every other weekend or so. But with Melon Days coming up, we're just going to hold off and skip this weekend since we'll be playing for the festival."

As they spoke, a white van pulled up, and a man and woman entered the drive-in, sitting in a nearby booth and studying the menu on the wall. They looked to be in their early forties, though the man was starting to go gray.

The pair was tanned and looked like they'd spent a good deal of time outdoors, nothing new for Green River, which saw a number of rafters, hikers, and climbers come to explore the river canyons and nearby San Rafael Swell.

The man was of average height and wore the ubiquitous jeans and t-shirt, but the woman was petite and had her dark brown hair pulled back with a colorful scarf. Her tan cargo pants and cotton shirt with its sleeves rolled up made her look like a desert commando, Bud thought, and he recognized the small bulge at her hip as probably being a concealed-carry handgun.

Turning to the woman, the man said, "Maddie, I noticed a sign for a grocery store down the street called the Melon Harvest. We should stop there and top everything up before we head out."

"Oh, Auggie, there'll be stores nearby. No need to get ahead of ourselves," the woman replied. "We need to get up there and set up."

Auggie replied, "I don't think there's anything nearby. It's out in the sticks, according to the map. I want to make us some good meals while we're out, and you know I need fresh stuff."

Howie asked, "If you don't mind my asking, where are you going? I'm the mayor here, and this guy across from me is the sheriff, and maybe we can answer any questions you have."

Maddie replied, "We're going to Joe's Valley."

"That's not far from Castle Dale," Howie replied. "They have an OK grocery store there. My ex-wife used to live there, though she lives here, now. She likes Green River better, since I'm here, no offense to Castle Dale."

Bud grinned. The pair had no way of knowing Maureen had divorced Howie, and they'd later remarried.

Maddie, looking perplexed, said, "She must be a bit conflicted. But we're just going camping for awhile."

"We're actually bear hunters," the man said, grinning. "Dire-bear hunters."

Maddie gave him an exasperated look, then added, "We need to place our order and be on our way, or we'll be setting up in the dark. Focus, Auggie."

"Have fun," Bud said, standing to leave, gathering up the mittens. "It's actually closer to the small town of Orangeville, which also has a grocery, but you do go through Castle Dale to get there. The valley's a beautiful place this time of year with the aspens turning."

With that, he was out the door, musing that one didn't see too many hunters in Green River, as the wildlife was more in the high country since most of the nearby area was desert. Once in awhile a hunter would come through on their way up into the Books or the Wasatch Plateau, and Joe's Valley was definitely bear country.

Heading across the street to his office, Bud wondered if the guy wasn't perhaps joking, for the pair sure didn't look like hunters, and was it even bear season? And had he meant they were hunting dire bears or that they were dire hunters looking for bears? If he remembered right, the museum up in Price had an impressive dire-bear skeleton on display with a placard that said dire bears had gone extinct some time ago.

As he unlocked the door to the small building that served as the Emery County Sheriff's office, he decided maybe it was time to talk to the state wildlife bunch and find out more about fox and bear hunting in Utah.

But first, he'd put the mittens in the safe until someone claimed them, then finish that article about photographing fireflies.

6

It was a couple of days later, and Bud sat in the sheriff's Land Cruiser, watching as a dark boiling mass made its way down the normally dry wash on the eastern edge of town. He knew it had to be pouring rain high in the Books, causing the wash to flash, the thick mixture of water, mud, and sticks eventually flowing to the river.

It reminded him of when the first head of water came down the farm ditches in the spring, though this wash was much bigger and deeper, a good twenty or thirty feet wide and ten feet deep, just one of many such waterways draining the Books.

He was soon on the phone, calling the railroad to tell them that the tracks could be compromised, as the wash ran up against the trackbed in places. He knew they would stop the trains, and once the flood had subsided, send out a truck to check the rails before letting any trains through.

Even though Green River was now primarily an agricultural town, trains had played a significant part in its history, the town having once been a layover for the Denver and Rio Grande Western Railroad, which built a station there in 1883. The arrival of the railroad resulted in the town becoming the scheduled meal stop for train passengers, and the town boomed for a decade until the railroad decided to transfer its operations north to the small town of Helper, named for the engines put on there to help the trains across Soldier Summit, the pass between Helper and Salt Lake City.

Bud thought again of Howie's saying about the more things change, and he knew Green River had certainly seen its share of change. Before the railroad arrived, a natural ford had served as a river crossing for the U.S. mail, eventually becoming the site of a ferry and stopover for travelers.

After the railroad boom, the area had stayed afloat economically from a uranium mill and also from the Green River Launch Complex, which shot Athena missiles to White Sands in New Mexico. When the complex was closed in 1974, the town's economy transformed into agriculture, primarily growing melons.

Now the head of the flashflood had moved past, the wash flowing with deep muddy water that Bud knew would probably soon subside, depending on how much rain the Books were getting. The big front Kale had mentioned had arrived, and as it started to sprinkle, he decided to go back to his office.

Driving past the Melon Rind Cafe, he noticed his manager Kale's pickup parked in front. Knowing the harvest was on hold because of the incoming storm, he decided to stop for a quick cup of coffee.

The cafe was full, and Kale and his wife Molly motioned for Bud to join them in their booth.

"Looks like the harvest is shut down," Bud said, sitting next to Molly as Maureen brought him a cup of coffee.

"We at least got that field of cantaloupe in," Kale replied, looking tired. "The crew worked until after dark, but it looks like we'll be shut down for awhile. This is supposed to be a wet one." He nodded at the cafe windows, where water was now streaming down, the rain setting in.

"You look like you could use a break," Bud replied, sipping the hot coffee.

"He can help me at the B&B," Molly replied. "I betcha anything we'll be full tonight. All those campers at the state park will be tired of getting wet."

"I thought you decided to shut down for the night," Kale replied. "Take a break after that last bunch."

"I can't turn away people in need," Molly replied. "Those guys weren't any trouble, I was just worried they'd get my foxes."

"Foxes?" Bud asked.

"There were four of 'em," Molly said. "Guys, not foxes. They were in some kind of club—one pair said they were from Salt Lake, another guy was from Alaska, and one was from Price. They were actually really nice fellows, and everything was going fine until I asked them what they were up to in Green River. I was just making small talk, like I do with all the guests. But when they told me they were fox hunting, I was ready to show them the door. I'll admit I got a little frosty with them after that, but they were leaving anyway."

"Were they driving a white SUV?" Bud asked.

"They were," Molly replied. "Along with a green pickup. And to think I was sittin' out on the back deck with them just the evening before when my little red foxes showed up. They thought they were the cutest things—and to think they hunt 'em. Despicable."

"Molly has a fox pair she feeds leftovers to," Kale added. "They're getting pretty tame."

"Oh, I know good and well I'm not supposed to feed the wildlife, Sheriff," she said. "But they keep the mice down."

"How can they keep the mice down when you're feeding them leftovers?" Kale asked. "Why would they want to hunt mice when they can have bacon and sausage?"

"I don't give them that much," Molly replied with frustration. "But I was glad when those fellows left, even though they were really nice, other than the fox hunting thing, anyway. They left a really nice tip."

"Did they say where they were going?" Bud asked.

Molly replied, "Yes, they said they were going up to Price, then on up the Wasatch Plateau. I asked if they knew about this bad weather coming in, and they said yes, but they just laughed and said a little rain wouldn't bother them, though it would probably hurt the propagation, whatever that meant."

Bud thought of the pair at Howie's the previous evening who had said they were going bear hunting. Was it possible they and the fox hunters knew each other?

Just then, Howie came through the door, water dripping from his rain jacket.

"You now have to call me General Howie," he said, holding up a piece of paper as he scooted in next to Kale.

"Why is that?" Molly asked. "Are you running away and joining the army?"

Howie laughed. "Because now I'm a general. I got my ham radio license, and I tested to the second highest level, which is general. I didn't even study."

"Congrats, General Mayor," Kale replied, grinning.

"How did you get it so fast?" Bud asked.

"They now let you test online," Howie replied as Maureen set a cup of coffee in front of him, squeezing his shoulder. "I was checking into it yesterday, and there's online testing, and Morse code's not required any more, so I signed up and took the test. I passed the first level, technician, so they asked if I wanted to try for the second level, which is general, and I passed that one, too. I'm going to keep studying for the highest level, which is amateur extra. The FCC emailed me my license this morning, and I printed it out."

"And what's this for exactly?" Molly asked.

"He's now legal to talk on the radio," Bud replied.

"I didn't know he was ever illegal," Molly laughed. "Is he starting a radio station in Green River? You could call it KMELON."

"You can only have four letters for a radio station," Howie said patiently. "But this is for ham radio, and you need a license to transmit. But Sheriff, this morning I was listening on that Yaesu you brought by, and I heard something kind of disturbing. I was going to call you."

"Disturbing?" Bud asked.

"I was listening to a net," Howie added, "Which is kind of like a club meeting, when someone broke in with an emergency. I didn't have a good signal, but the net manager said someone needing medical help was stuck up above Joe's Valley. The signal dropped, and he said he was going to contact the sheriff."

"I haven't heard from anyone," Bud replied. "Though I would suspect they would contact the sheriff for Carbon County up in Price, as it's closer. But the roads up on the plateau are going to be pretty much impassible, depending on exactly where they are. It's a big area."

"This storm's just getting started," Kale said. "It's supposed to rain for the next day, and it could be snowing up there."

"I don't think there's much we can do," Bud replied with worry. "But I'm going to get back to the office. I'll call Sheriff Davis in Price."

"I'll come with," Howie said. "Maybe we should head over to Castle Dale, just in case."

"Might be a good idea," Bud replied, scooting out of the booth, coffee cup still in hand. "I need to contact search and rescue and see if anyone over there knows anything. Maybe we can get up into the high country before the roads get too bad."

"They have to *already* be bad," Molly said. "Or they wouldn't be stuck."

"True," Bud replied. "And it probably wouldn't be a bad idea to check on that couple who was going to camp in Joe's Valley. It could even be them."

"If so, I bet they have some good cuss words for my list," Howie said.

"I doubt if they'd be grandma approved," Bud replied as they went out the door. "And it seems odd that all of a sudden everyone has ham radios, doesn't it?"

"Let's go find their QTH," Howie replied. "That's ham talk for location. I'm going to bring that HT you found. I made two battery banks for it, so it should last awhile."

"Roger that," Bud replied as they walked out the door into the pouring rain. "I still have those mittens. Maybe we can find their owner."

7

Bud and Howie sat in front of the gas-log fireplace in the house Bud's wife had recently acquired in the coal-mining town of Price, a good hour to the north of Green River. Lindie was stretched out in front of the fire, sleeping, her legs twitching as if chasing a rabbit while Howie fiddled with the radio Bud had found.

The house had originally been part of a trade Wilma Jean had made for her cafe, but she'd managed to eventually buy the cafe back and keep the house, which they'd fixed up. It had once belonged to Bud's grandparents, and it was still somewhat of a shock to him that it was back in the family.

It served as a handy retreat any time they were in the area, and he and Howie were happy to have its comfort, as it had rained so hard on the way up that they'd foregone taking the unpaved Green River cutoff across the Swell to Castle Dale and decided to come the long way around through Price.

"You guys really fixed this place up," Howie remarked, munching on a roast-beef sandwich he'd brought with him from his drive-in, Lindie now awake and begging.

"We had a lot of help," Bud remarked. "But it turned out really nice, didn't it? Wilma Jean's pretty good at creating comfy spaces."

"I still think it's great you were able to get your grandparents' old house," Howie replied. "But who was that who just called?"

"It was Mrs. Jensen. I redirected the sheriff's 911 line to the State Patrol, but she called on my cell phone. She said she needed help getting Frosty out of the couch."

"Don't you mean *off* the couch?"

"No, she said he was stuck in their pull-out sofa. I told her to call the fire department, but she said Frosty didn't want her to, as he'd be the laughing stock of the town."

"For real? How'd he get stuck in the sofa?" Howie asked with concern.

"She said he'd pulled it open to work on the mechanism and it had closed up with him in it. I could hear him laughing in the background, so I wasn't too worried. He managed to get himself out as we were talking. She said to come by when we get back and get some snickerdoodle cookies, as she's just baked a fresh batch."

"Sounds good," Howie said. "And the SAR bunch you talked to hadn't heard anything about someone stuck up on the plateau?"

"No, and neither had Carbon County Sheriff Davis or anyone around here or Castle Dale. I'm not sure what we can do at this point, Howie, especially with this storm setting in."

"It's raining so hard we would drive right by someone stuck and not even see them," Howie replied. "Or maybe drive right over them —or get stuck ourselves. It's kind of nice just hanging around here, nice and cozy, nobody to bother us."

"You get a lot of people bothering you as mayor?" Bud kidded.

"You'd be surprised," Howie replied. "Probably kind of like you do as sheriff, though for different reasons. And the drive-in gets pretty hectic. I wouldn't have been able to leave today if my helper wasn't there. But Sheriff, did you hear about the two ham antennas that got married? The ceremony wasn't much, but the reception was excellent."

Bud groaned as Howie added, "Hams can be real hams, but in a dad jokes kind of way. Anyway, Maureen told me that it was either her or the radio, over."

He paused, waiting, then added, "Get it? Over, like I chose the radio. OK, never mind, another bad joke."

He sighed, then continued. "Bud, sometimes I just want to run wild and be free. I get tired of being responsible. When I tried to talk to Maureen about it the other day, she said that the blow to my head when Bodie knocked the shelf down maybe did something to me."

"Sounds like burn-out to me, Howie. Maybe getting back into radio will help you get out and about more, at least mentally."

Scooting his chair closer to the fireplace, Howie asked, "Would you like to hear why I gave up ham radio when I was younger? I mean, it's kind of a weird story. I've never really talked about it to anyone, as I didn't want to come off as being superstitious."

"You're the last person I would suspect of being superstitious, Howie. You're too scientific. You're always looking for the answer, no matter what. To most of us, radio waves are a form of magic, but you're like a wizard who understands them."

"Well, my brain does kind of work in mysterious ways, I guess," Howie replied. "I've always felt there was an answer for about everything, if we could just figure it out. But this one's been beyond me, and I mean it's been beyond me for a long time. I sold my radio gear after this happened. I'd just graduated from high school."

"It must've been pretty serious for you to do that."

"I don't know, but it felt that way. Anyway, this happened up on the shore of Scofield Reservoir, not all that far from here. I was with my dad, who was fishing, and I was messing around with my radio. I'd set up a makeshift antenna, a homemade dipole, and I was doing pretty well with it, making a few contacts, just talking while Dad fished. I thought ham radio was great fun—a way to get away from real people to talk to people I couldn't see. It was a bright sunny afternoon, not at all cloudy and foggy, like one might expect for a story like this."

Howie paused, gazing into the fireplace, then continued in a voice so low Bud had to struggle to hear him.

"This woman who said her name was Lydia Scott came on the air, and she talked about her life. It was really interesting."

"Like what?"

"Well, for example, she said she had grown up in the town of Scofield, and her family had all come from Finland to work in the coal mines, including her husband. As you know, Scofield's not much of a town, and to grow up there is a lot like growing up in my hometown of Sunnyside, though Scofield's even smaller. I mentioned this, and she said she'd never heard of Sunnyside, which I found strange, as Scofield's almost a ghost town and Sunnyside has several hundred people, and both are coal-mining towns, or were, anyway."

"So, after we talked for awhile, she asked me what my QTH was, and I told her I was at the reservoir, then asked where she was. She replied that she'd never heard of the reservoir, then she started crying, right there on the radio. I found it really odd, and I tried to reassure her, asking if there was anything I could help her with."

"She finally apologized, saying she'd just lost her husband and two sons at the mine cave-in. I was puzzled, as there hadn't been any recent cave-ins that I'd heard about, though there have been a few historically in that area. I told her I was really sorry, then asked what mine, and she said Winter Quarters, then the signal faded and all I got was static after that."

"Anyway, Sheriff, like I said, it was a beautiful sunny day, but I felt this incredible sense of foreboding. I decided to find my dad and see if we could go home. As I was gathering up my antenna and gear, this fisherman guy came by and saw my radio and asked what I was doing. I told him I was a ham, and he asked who I'd been talking to."

"I found that kind of odd, because I'd never had anyone ask who I'd been talking to on the radio, 'cause with a ham, the odds are good it's someone you've never met in another state or even in another country. I told him I'd been having a conversation with a woman named Lydia, and he asked if her name was Lydia Scott and was she from Scofield and then mentioned stuff he wouldn't have necessarily known without knowing her. I asked him if he was a ham and had maybe talked to her in the past, and he said no, but lots of people had talked to Lydia, and some had even met her there on the lake shore."

"By then, I had everything put away and couldn't wait to get out of there, so I started saying goodbye to the fellow, but as I walked away, he told me Lydia Scott died in 1910 of heartbreak, as her family had been killed in the big Winter Quarters Mine disaster that killed over 200 miners in 1900, some of them just kids. Then he added that she was seen and heard a lot around Scofield, and the townspeople were pretty weirded out by it. She was always on 14.313 MHz. Bud, that's exactly the frequency we were talking on. How could he have known that?"

"So, I walked back to the car and got in and waited for my dad to show up, and it still gives me chills to think about it. I tried to brush it off as a joke, and I later looked through some of the old newspapers from that time on microfiche at the library, but I wasn't able to find her obituary. But I did learn that in 1900, Scofield had 1800 inhabitants, and Sunnyside wasn't even really a town, just a bunch of tents and a few houses. Scofield Reservoir wasn't built until 1926. The Winter Quarters mine had a lot of Finns working there, and around 150 of the miners from the Winter Quarters disaster are buried at the Scofield cemetery, which is only two miles from the reservoir."

"Howie, it had to have been a joke," Bud replied. "This Lydia person and probably her brother or someone she knew were playing a trick on whoever might be listening in."

"I went through all that in my mind, Bud, but what are the odds of me being there with a radio and picking up her signal at that specific time on that specific day? Slim to none. And what would be their motive?"

"Maybe it was a skip through time," Bud replied. "Maybe you cracked the time-travel nut. You should get back on the radio and see if you can conjure up Marconi—didn't he invent the radio?"

Howie laughed, pushing his chair back.

"So you really think it was a prank?" Howie asked.

"I'm not sure, but that would be my first guess," Bud answered. "Especially given how the guy asked who you'd been talking to on the radio. Seems odd. And Howie, Scott's not a Finnish name, as far as I know."

They sat in silence for awhile, watching the fireplace, until finally,

Bud said, "Howie, this rain's not going to let up, so we might as well go on up to Joe's Valley. The SAR bunch hasn't had any luck, and I doubt if we will, either. Let's stop and get a few supplies then drive up there, go as far as the road lets us, then go on home. At least we'll have tried."

"Sounds good," Howie replied.

"But first," Bud added. "I'd like to make a quick stop at the museum and visit their dire-bear display."

"Why?" Howie asked.

"I'm just curious about dire bears, as that one couple said they were going dire-bear hunting. I thought maybe the display would have something helpful."

"I'm always up for visiting dire bears," Howie laughed as they put on their raincoats. "As long as they're not alive—and don't eat radios."

8

Bud stood in front of the skeleton of an imposing-looking creature, its shoulders easily as tall as his head, a nearby sign calling it a short-nose bear, or dire bear. Nearby, the towering skeleton of a mammoth dwarfed both him and the bear.

A placard by the bear read:

Arctodus simus, the giant short-faced bear or dire bear, averaged 2,000 pounds and stood six-feet tall at the shoulder. When standing on its hind legs, these massive bears could reach up to 12 feet in height. The species first appeared roughly 800,000 years ago in what is now the United States, and soon spread into Canada.

The dire bear's size worked against it, as its inability to turn quickly made it a poor ambush predator. It is thought that the bear plodded along after its prey, wearing it down with its superior endurance. It may have also bullied other predators into giving up their catches.

The nearby Columbian mammoth skeleton comes from a cave near Huntington Reservoir and has dire-bear gnaw marks, with an Arctodus specimen preserved in association with its remains. It's the youngest dated dire-bear skeleton found to date, making scientists believe it was one of the last bears of its species before it went extinct. It is thought that the central

and southern plateaus of the Rocky Mountains acted as a refuge for Ice Age
megafauna, which included dire wolves, ground sloths, shrub-ox, prong-
horns, horses, lynx, pumas, black bears, mountain goats, and vampire bats.
The region has yielded some of the largest specimens of dire bears,
including what was once the largest specimen on record, found in the Salt
Lake Valley. The plateaus received more rainfall during the Late Pleis-
tocene, as glacially cooled air collided with hot desert air which resulted in
a wide range of parklands and woodlands.

Bud stood for some time, lost in the thought that his beloved
desert had once been home to such creatures, although he knew the
nearby Wasatch Plateau must have been more the center of their
habitat, being at a higher altitude. The small town of Huntington was
a mere 20 miles or so south, with the reservoir nearby, on the flanks
of the plateau.

The cool rainy day made the museum feel chilly, and the thought
of meeting a dire bear made him feel even chillier. Was this what
Auggie and Maddie were looking for? They'd said they were dire-
bear hunting, and they were going to Joe's Valley, which cut into the
edge of the plateau just a short distance south of Huntington. Were
they paleontologists, or were they illegal fossil diggers? A dire-bear
skeleton would be potentially worth a million dollars or more to the
right collector.

He walked around for a few minutes, looking at several displays
of dinosaur bones that had been found in the area. Howie waited in
the FJ, as he'd wanted to check out the radio, now that he had his
license and could transmit legally.

Putting a few dollars in the donation box, Bud went back outside,
surprised to see the rain had let up, though it was still gray and
cloudy.

Lindie, who was looking out the FJ's back window, began wagging
her tail, and as Bud got into the FJ, he heard Howie say, "I sure hope
your wife gets home soon, Jim, and you can get back to normal food.
It's kind of interesting you were just in Green River. Back to you. This
is WØRQC."

A voice replied, "Roger that, WØRQC. We had a good time down there. I'm sure you know it's National Fox-Hunting Month. A lot of the clubs are getting together. Anyway, sure has been nice ragchewing with you. Where did you say your QTH was? Over."

"At this moment, I'm in the parking lot at the museum in Price, but it looks like we'll be heading out soon," Howie replied.

"The museum? No kidding? That's where I'm at. I'm the education coordinator, and I'm upstairs in my office taking a break. What a coincidence! No wonder we have such a good signal. I'm looking out my window as we speak. Are you in the brown pickup with the white topper? KFØSTL over."

Howie continued. "No, Jim, we're in the FJ, just heading out. Be sure to stop by next time you're in Green River. Over."

"I'll do that. We had a good time down there yesterday fox hunting. 73 and clear."

"WØRQC clear."

Bud, who was backing out, could see what looked like the brown pickup he'd seen when leaving Tusher Canyon, and with its Saskatchewan plate, he was sure it was one and the same.

It was unusual, but not necessarily out of the ordinary, he thought, to see the same vehicle in different towns, especially if they were tourists. The museum was well-known, and though Tusher Canyon was off the beaten path, if one asked a local about places to see petroglyphs it would come up. Green River and Price weren't that far from each other, and a tourist could easily be visiting both.

As he watched, someone got out of the pickup and headed for the museum. They wore a baseball cap and what looked like a sheepskin jacket, though Bud couldn't make out much, other than that they were small and thin.

"Ask him if they found any foxes," Bud asked. "I thought I recognized his callsign. KFØSTL was one of the guys who called on the radio as I was coming out of the canyon. What does 73 mean, and why do you use your callsigns so much?"

"73 is short for best wishes," Howie replied. "Lots of the ham stuff is from the old days of the teletype when they shortened everything up as much as possible. The FCC requires you to repeat your callsign every 10 minutes as well as when you sign off."

Bud noted the person from the pickup had stopped and turned around as if noticing the FJ, possibly recognizing it from Tusher Canyon.

He could now see that they wore reflective sunglasses and had their coat collar pulled up along their chin as if to not be recognized.

"Does that look like it could be a woman to you, Howie?" Bud asked.

"Maybe, but it's hard to tell the way they're all covered up."

"Do you think they're trying to go stealth?"

"Could be, Sheriff. Wearing sunglasses on a rainy day like this is about as useless as screen doors on a submarine, so why else unless they're trying to go incognito? And look how they have their hat pulled down and their collar pulled up. Maybe they're going to rob the museum. Should we stick around?"

"I don't think they would get much," Bud replied. "The donation box was almost empty."

After pulling out onto the street, he glanced back, only to see the person had turned around and was getting into their pickup, which seemed odd.

"Howie, let's stop at the grocery store, then get going before the rain sets back in," Bud said, watching as the truck pulled out onto the street a few cars behind them.

"That's a Roger," Howie replied. "Let's go. WØRQC clear."

"I hope we actually are clear," Bud replied with concern, wondering if the pickup might be following them.

They would find out soon enough, he decided.

9

After stopping at the grocery store, Bud and Howie were soon on Highway 10, going south through a wide plain between the San Rafael Swell and the Wasatch Plateau, though not much was visible in the rain.

"Ford Ridge is way up there," Howie said, pointing into the mist. "There's a repeater up on top."

"I really don't know what we're going to be able to do in this rain," Bud replied. "Once we get to the reservoir, the roads are going to turn to gravel and then mud."

They soon passed through the small town of Huntington, which set at the mouth of the same canyon that held the site where the mammoth and dire-bear skeletons in the Price museum had been found.

The next town was Castle Dale, and Bud turned onto a shortcut that bypassed the town, heading west, and they were soon in what was known as Left Fork or Straight Canyon, leaving the lower country for the montane landscape of the Manti–La Sal National Forest that covered the Wasatch Plateau.

It wasn't long before they were in the sagebrush-covered flats of Joe's Valley, surrounded by tall slopes covered in aspen and pinion pines and littered with large boulders that were home to bouldering areas with names like *Kill by Numbers* and *Beyond Life*.

Turning to look over his shoulder, Howie said, "Bud, I think that pickup's following us. I've been keeping an eye out, and it seems to stay just far enough behind that we won't notice it, but a few times it's gotten closer."

"I've noticed it too, Howie," Bud replied. "It's that same one we saw at the museum, the one with Saskatchewan plates. It's easier to spot now that the rain's lifting."

They had reached the long wedge-shaped Joe's Valley Reservoir and were now driving along its shore, soon coming to a series of buildings with the sign *Joe's Valley Resort and Marina*. An elderly couple sat under the awning of one of the cabins, waving congenially as Bud and Howie passed.

"That pickup's no longer making an effort to hide," Howie said as Bud slowed.

"We'll ditch them at the campground," Bud replied. "We can park in the trees. The rain's stopped, so we can take Lindie for a walk and see if there's anyone around who might know about that rescue call."

Bud quickly pulled into a campground near the reservoir, tucking the FJ into a site surrounded by juniper and pinions. They waited, Bud finally saying, "I think they must be on past us."

Putting Lindie on a leash, they began walking around the campground, which appeared to be deserted.

"Everyone with any sense has gone home," Howie said. "No fun camping in a downpour, plus it's cold."

"Autumn's pretty much here, Howie," Bud replied. "Which makes me even more anxious about a report that someone's out here needing medical help. But at this point, they've either found help or... well, I hate to think about the alternative."

"Don't look now, Sheriff, but that pickup seems to have found us," Howie said as the brown pickup with the white topper pulled up next to them, its Saskatchewan plates half-covered with mud.

An older woman rolled down the pickup window, and Bud thought she looked weary.

"Can we help you?" Bud asked, noting how tiny his reflection looked in the amber-colored lenses of her sunglasses.

"Where's Cy and Christian?" she asked, gray hair sticking out from under her baseball cap.

"Cy and Christian?" Bud asked, puzzled. "I'm not sure who you're asking about. I did meet a fellow named Christian back in a cafe in Green River, but that was several days ago."

"That was Christian, and his grandfather, Cy, is with him. They're my grandson and husband. I need to find them."

"And you're thinking they're clear over here?" Bud asked. "Seems like Christian said something about going to Delta, if that helps. Why would they be over here? This is the wrong direction for Delta."

"Look," the woman replied, clearly irritated. "I know they're around here somewhere, and they appear to be traveling with you. I saw you over in that canyon by Green River, and I know they were with you, as well as at the museum back in Price. They can't hide from me forever."

"Why would they want to hide from their own family?" Howie asked. "It's none of my business, but are you having some kind of spat or something? But honestly, we haven't seen hide nor hair of them. You do know you're talking to the county sheriff here, right?" He nodded at Bud.

"My name's Elizabeth Walker," she said quietly, though still obviously irritated. "I don't mean to be contentious, Sheriff, but you do realize you're aiding and abetting a criminal by helping my husband?"

"How is he a criminal?" Howie asked.

"And who are *you* exactly?" Elizabeth asked.

"Howie McPherson," Howie replied.

Bud was surprised Howie didn't mention he was the mayor of Green River, but he decided maybe he was purposely lying low until things got sorted out.

"My husband took something from a museum in Canada," Elizabeth replied.

"And you're following him around trying to get it back?" Howie asked.

"Are you the county barrister or something?" Elizabeth asked. "Attorney or whatever you call it here in the States? And for the record, no, I'm not following him around—or wasn't anyway. I spend part of the year with Christian and his family in Salt Lake City, seeing my great-grandkids. I'm allowed to stay six months by U.S. law. Cy always stays home, but this time he came down totally unannounced. He thinks you can still cross the border using your driver's license, like in the old days."

"So he's here illegally?" Bud asked.

As if suddenly realizing what she was saying, Elizabeth said, "No, no, he's perfectly legal. He has a driver's license."

"What did he take?" Howie asked as Elizabeth started up her pickup to leave.

She replied, "He has something that belongs to the museum. My grandmother was from Great Britain. She emigrated to Canada and married my grandfather, a Cree. Her name was Elizabeth. She was named for the queen, and I was named for her. She left something important to me, and I gave it to the museum on loan, but Cy thinks it has something that will lead him to the Grandfathers, so he took it. He says it holds some kind of important secret."

"But what is it?" Howie asked. "And who are the Grandfathers?"

"You can ask Cy, since you know where he is," she answered. "But I'll keep looking, and I can guarantee I'll find them. I have an infallible method, thanks to Christian's Kraken."

"Kraken?" Howie repeated. "What's a kraken?"

"You ask too many questions," Elizabeth replied.

Bud said, "We're here investigating a report of someone stuck up on the plateau who needs medical attention. We really know nothing about your family's whereabouts, but maybe it's them. Does you husband have a medical condition?"

Now looking concerned, she said, "Yes, Cy has a bad heart. He's on a big handful of medications. Oh lord, I hope they're OK. Please tell me where they are."

"But I thought you had an infallible method of finding them," Howie said. "Why don't you share that with us so we can help look?"

"I've already said too much," she replied, slowly backing the truck. "I'm going to get my husband in trouble."

"How did he get into the States without a passport?" Bud asked.

"He said he walked across the border dressed as a bear," she replied. "Knowing him, it's true. But where does this road go? They were here with you and must've gone on up this road."

"It eventually goes all the way across the plateau," Bud replied. "But it's not paved, and you'll be stuck before you get very far."

As she turned the truck around and started to leave, Howie asked her, "What makes you think they're with us?"

"A little birdie told me," she replied, then was gone, heading up the very road Bud had told her not to take.

10

"Welcome to the Dire Bear Cafe," Auggie said, placing a pan of freshly baked cinnamon rolls on the worn wooden table where Bud and Howie sat.

The small dark-haired woman named Maddie sat at the end of the table, which was strewn with maps, books, a laptop computer, and various notebooks. Several shovels and digging implements leaned near the door, along with two pair of muddy boots.

"This place is way nicer than I thought it would be," Bud said as Auggie dished out a gooey roll onto a plate in front of him. "I've been by here many times, but never inside. I bet Orange Olsen had no idea his Forest Service house would turn into a place the locals rent for a few days just to get away and fish at the lake. Running water, indoor plumbing, a nice big fridge—it looks like I imagine it did when he lived here."

Bud and Howie had followed Elizabeth up the road past the campground, but had stopped at the end of the pavement, where two old white clapboard houses sat in an open sagebrush meadow dotted with pinion-juniper and ponderosa pines. The houses had been built years ago by the Forest Service, and one could make out the reservoir in the distance.

Elizabeth had continued on up the hill, though they suspected they would be seeing her on foot before long, her pickup stuck. Seeing what appeared to be the same white van that had been at Howie's Drive-In, though now mud-splattered, they had decided to stop and ask if Maddie and Auggie knew anything about a possible medical emergency.

Maddie, moving a stack of books so Auggie could put the pan down, replied, "We rented this place for a month. Did you see the commemorative plaque out in the yard? It says Orange Olsen was born in 1890 and died in 1945. I wonder what happened to him, as that would make him only fifty-five when he died. Was he related to whoever they named the nearby town of Orangeville after?"

"Yes, that was his grandfather, Orange Seely, one of the area's early pioneer settlers," Bud replied. "Orange Olsen lived in this house when he worked for the forest service. He pioneered the aerial tracking of big game populations for census purposes. He was a staunch conservationist and died in an airplane crash while conducting an aerial count of elk."

"That's a real shame," Auggie said, lighting a propane heater in the center of the living room. "The rain's stopped, but it's chilly in here. I just put on a fresh pot of coffee. We're here on a dig."

Howie nodded amiably, picking up a book with the title, *Vertebrate Paleontology in Utah*. "I'll take a cup, thanks very much. I take it you're paleontologists?"

"Good guess," Maddie replied. "We're affiliated with the University of Utah. We both teach there, but we're currently on sabbatical to research Pleistocene megafauna on the Wasatch Plateau. A rock climber found what look like dire-bear bones in a nearby cave."

"Joe's Valley is definitely a rock-climber's paradise," Howie said. "It's pretty famous for bouldering with its huge sandstone rocks everywhere, and I'm not surprised that those rocks guard fossils."

Maddie replied, "The cave's off the beaten path, and I hope nobody bothers us. We'd prefer it stays unknown."

"Is it easy to get to from here?" Howie asked.

"It's not bad," she replied. "It's pretty hidden up in the trees. But have you heard a current weather report? I'm wondering how much longer before it dries up so we can get up there."

"It's supposed to be clearing," Bud said. "But have you seen anyone come by recently? We have word that someone's stuck up here and may need medical attention."

Auggie placed cups in front of everyone, then set to pouring coffee from an old stainless-steel percolator pot, as Maddie said, "There were two guys who came by yesterday in a Chevy Silverado. They didn't stop. We never saw them come back down, but we weren't sitting around watching, either. Maybe they went on over to the other side of the plateau."

"They're probably stuck up there, is more like it," Howie replied.

"Is there any way to get to them if they are?" Maddie asked.

"Not until things dry up," Howie replied. "But do you have any idea what a kraken is?"

"A kraken?" Auggie asked. "What made you think of a kraken?"

"Well," Howie replied. "We were talking to this woman who said she had a kraken. It seems vaguely familiar, but I can't place it."

"The kraken is an enormous mythical sea monster said to appear off the coast of Norway," Maddie answered. "I remember reading about it once in an undergrad class in mythology, but that's all I know. I remember it because the book had this impressive drawing of a huge squid wrapped around a big sailboat. But why would anyone be talking about a kraken out here? We're thousands of miles from the ocean."

"Maybe there's one in the reservoir," Howie replied.

"How would it get here from Norway?" Auggie asked.

Howie replied, "Maybe it was in a barrel brought in by settlers, you know, a little one, a baby kraken, accidentally in some saltwater, like in a barrel of pickles or something. The reservoir's over 250 feet deep, so a kraken would have lots of room to grow, though it would probably get lonely."

Bud, who'd been flipping through a book called *Ancient Landscapes of the Colorado Plateau*, looked up.

"How would that work when the reservoir is freshwater and wasn't built until the 1960s, Howie?"

"Do you know any good cuss words?" Howie changed the subject. "Ones that are grandma safe."

"She knows some humdingers," Auggie replied. "And none are grandma safe. Most aren't even grandpa safe."

"Any examples?" Howie asked.

"Well, I say crikey a lot," Auggie replied. "But I won't repeat Maddie's vast repertoire of cuss words. She's an expert."

"Cussing is good for your mental health," Maddie said. "It helps release anger."

"She calls me a chucklehead occasionally," Auggie said pensively. "But that's about as tame as she gets. But why do you ask?"

"Just a little project I've got going," Howie replied.

Just then, someone tapped on the door, and as Auggie opened it, Bud could see it was Elizabeth, which didn't surprise him. Her boots were covered with thick mud, and as she bent over to take them off, she muttered, "I've never seen mud so sticky."

"Did you get stuck?" Howie asked.

"I did, but I managed to get out. But I found where Cy and Christian got stuck, though they appear to have gotten unstuck and kept going, because their truck's nowhere in sight."

"How do you know it was them?" Bud asked.

Elizabeth took something from her shirt pocket and held it up.

"This blue feather is from Christian's fancy dancer outfit. It was on the ground where they got stuck. But there's something else— another vehicle was up there after they were, by the looks of the tracks. Someone was following them, which explains why they didn't turn around."

"He's a fancy dancer?" Maddie asked. "Like in powwows?"

"Exactly," Elizabeth replied. "Christian's a top-rated fancy dancer, and they were on their way to the powwow in Delta. I have no idea why they're clear over here, and I don't understand why the signal was coming from you guys." She looked intently at Bud and Howie, then added, "But I have a bad feeling about all this. It looks like they're being followed by someone else, and I'm really worried about them, especially given Cy's health problems. Isn't there anything we can do?"

Bud stood, saying, "It's getting dark, and there's no way we can search for them with the roads mudded in. I need to get back home, but I'll organize a search party for them tomorrow. In the meantime, if they happen to get themselves out, let me know."

He handed Maddie a card with his phone number, then added, "And Elizabeth, maybe you could stay in the area so we can meet up in the morning. Do you have a cell phone?"

She replied, "No cell phone, and no money. I was supposed to be going back to Salt Lake today."

"You can stay here," Maddie said. "This place has only two bedrooms, but mine has bunkbeds. I have an extra sleeping bag, since you have to supply your own bedding. Auggie will be fixing dinner soon, so you'll be fine until tomorrow."

"Dinner at the Dire Bear Cafe—we're having fried potatoes and spam with my special hot sauce, a nice salad, and chocolate ice cream for dessert," Auggie added.

"Auggie loves to cook," Maddie added. "You'll eat well here, considering we're basically camping." Nodding toward Bud and Howie, she added, "You guys are welcome to stay for dinner."

But Bud and Howie were already half out at the door, Lindie at their heels, thanking them, but eager to get back to Green River.

11

Bud woke with a start, not sure where he was for a few moments until it gradually dawned on him that he was home in his own bed with Wilma Jean breathing softly at his side. Wiener dog Pierre was buried down under the covers, Hoppie snored at Bud's feet, and Lindie was curled up in her big fluffy doughnut-bed on the floor.

It was still dark outside, though the alarm clock said it was almost six a.m., so he knew the sun was on its way, soon to light up the huge palisades of the Books above town, as the storm had blown over, taking the clouds away.

He felt tense and uneasy as if something was wrong, but the dogs were all asleep, so the odds were good nothing was going on, as they were good watchdogs—or was that just when they were awake? Whatever had awakened him, it had left him with an unsettled feeling, and he knew his best course of action was to do nothing until he identified the threat.

Lying very still, he finally began drifting back asleep, then once again jerked awake. This time, he knew what was going on, for the image seared across his mind left no room for doubt—a giant squid-like creature was wrapped around his FJ, trying to get inside while he and the dogs cowered in fear, windows rolled up, wondering if it was able to break the glass.

It had been a dream—a dream that seemed so real that it prompted him to slip out of bed and peek through the living-room windows to see if his FJ was still parked out by the front gate.

Hoppie and Lindie were at his side, wanting out, Pierre still in bed under the covers, unaware that the world was turning without him.

Bud hesitated for a moment, then turned on the deck light and opened the door, letting them out into the yard, still uncertain whether or not it was safe, though he knew it had been just a dream.

He watched the dogs nose around the grass for a moment, then went into the kitchen and started a pot of percolator coffee, the strange feeling gradually lifting as he began to fully wake up.

Coffee ready, he poured a cup, added a dollop of vanilla-bean ice cream, let the dogs back inside, gave them each a Barkie Biscuit, then made himself comfortable in his big recliner, opening his laptop.

Thinking back on what Elizabeth had said about having something called a kraken, he did a search, then read:

> The kraken is a legendary sea monster that appears in the sea between Norway and Iceland, a huge creature with a reputation for pulling down ships. It is believed that the legend of the kraken may have originated from sightings of giant squids, which may grow to 34 feet in length. It was first described in 1734 in detail by explorer Hans Egede, a Norwegian explorer. Writer Jules Verne depicted the kraken in his novels.

Closing the laptop, he leaned back, wondering why Elizabeth had mentioned having such a thing. She seemed sure that she would find her husband, saying that she had Christian's kraken, which was "an infallible method."

Bud finished his coffee, thinking back on the previous day up at Joe's Valley. He and Howie had toyed with the idea of staying in the house in Price for the night, since they'd be going back to look for Cy and Christian, but he was anxious to see Wilma Jean and the pups, plus he needed to make sure nothing of any importance had happened in his absence. Howie was also anxious to get home, so they'd stayed the course and driven on back to Green River.

As they'd made their way home, they'd discussed how to effectively conduct a search for Cy and Christian when the roads were probably still impassable. Howie had suggested an air search, and Bud had later asked Wilma Jean if she could fly them in her little Cessna over the plateau the next day, which she'd agreed to do.

They could cover a lot of ground that way in a short time, which would be a good thing, especially if Cy was having medical issues.

Bud knew that the upcoming flight was part of the reason he'd had unsettled dreams, for he wasn't fond of flying, especially at the low altitude they'd have to maintain to conduct an effective search. The idea made him queasy, and he went back into the kitchen and refilled his coffee cup, adding an especially large dollop of ice cream.

Sitting back down in his recliner, he wondered why Christian and Cy were up on the plateau, especially since they'd said they were on their way to Delta. Was Christian's grandfather looking for more of what he called the Grandfathers, which Bud assumed was rock art?

Elizabeth had said the blue feathers were part of Christian's outfit as a well-known fancy dancer, and that they were headed to the powwow in Delta, and yet they were now way off-course over on the Wasatch Plateau.

He again opened the laptop, this time keying in the words *fancy dancer*:

The Fancy Dance, or Fancy War Dance, is a style of dance created by the Ponca tribe in the 1920s in an attempt to preserve their culture and religion and is loosely based on the war dance. It has spread far beyond the Ponca and is now performed by various Native American tribes at powwows, the movements of the dancer timed perfectly to the beat of a drum. This dance is very flashy and colorful and requires stamina, strength, and coordination.

Bud closed his laptop, getting up and going out onto the back deck with the dogs at his heels. The first hints of dawn now lit up the distant Books, and he knew Wilma Jean would soon be up. He wasn't sure how soon she would want to get going, as it was possible she'd want to wait out the early morning air currents and fly when things were more stable.

Maybe he'd have time to recruit someone else to fly in his place, maybe his good friend Shorty. Howie had already said he would like to go, and his and Shorty's eyes were as good as Bud's. He could drive on over there and meet them at the Price airport when the search was done.

His kraken dream had mostly faded away, but he again looked out to make sure his FJ didn't have a giant squid wrapped around it. All was fine, except for the small bunny sitting by the front wheel, munching on a stalk of alfalfa.

Bud smiled. The dogs were always patrolling the yard for rabbits, never seeing any, but now they slept as this interloper enjoyed breakfast in full sight.

Still feeling a bit unsettled, he went back inside, sat back down, yet again opened his laptop, and keyed in the words *kraken locator:*

The KrakenSDR is a radio receiver that can locate any transmission source between 100 MHz to 1 GHz. It works with mapping software and a set of magnet mount antennas. It can literally locate a transmitter in a few seconds. Mount the antennas on your vehicle, start the KrakenSDR software and mapping app, then drive until the mapping software pinpoints the transmitter. It will provide turn by turn directions.

Some uses include 1) physically locating an unknown transmitter of interest such as one doing illegal broadcasts; 2) performing ham radio experiments such as monitoring repeater abuse; and 3) locating lost ships via VHF radio.

The most common application that the KrakenSDR is used for is radio direction finding, or determining the directional bearing of an RF transmitter. By taking multiple bearing readings with various antennas one can triangulate the location of the transmitter.

Bingo! So, a device called a kraken actually existed, Bud mused, possibly named for its ability to find lost ships, ships theoretically wrecked by the kraken sea monster. Elizabeth had one of these devices, and it was letting her track the radio Howie was using—Christian's radio.

That would explain why she thought Cy and Christian were with them, for every time Howie transmitted on it, she picked up the signal, thinking it was Christian.

He leaned back, feeling like he'd solved that small mystery, until he wondered how she was able to distinguish Howie's signal from anyone else's. Didn't all radios put out pretty much the same type of signal when it came to transmitting? And what had she meant when she'd said a little birdie had told her where they were, even though she'd said she had a kraken. Did Christian's radio sound like a bird when transmitting, and how would that work?

Feeling like he was getting nowhere, Bud closed the laptop, fed the dogs their breakfast, then headed for the shower.

He would get around before his wife got up, then make a quick phone call, seeing if his geologist friend Shorty was interested in a recon flight over the Wasatch Plateau.

He was beginning to feel that time was of the essence, especially given how long Cy and Christian had been gone. He thought back to the vehicles Gord had seen up Tusher Canyon and wondered if they had anything to do with it all.

If Shorty would go along with them, he could drive his FJ to Price and meet them at the airport, and they would then have a vehicle, which they would need. Wilma Jean could fly on back to Green River, and they could go meet up with Elizabeth at what he was now beginning to think of as the Dire Bear Cafe.

He knew the roads across the plateau would be drying up, and he hoped that the enterprise would end in a rescue, and he could then get back to important things like the watermelon harvest. He was beginning to miss the peace and quiet of Green River, as well as sitting under the big cottonwood on the farm, wondering if he should go wander.

What was the word Gord had taught him? Juoksentelisinkohan—

YOKE-sen-TELL-ee-seen-ko-hahn. Given the size of Emery County, which was his jurisdiction as sheriff, including the part of the Wasatch Plateau where Christian and Cy were apparently lost, he knew he could be set for lots of wandering until they were found, which he hoped would be soon.

12

Bud sat in front of the fireplace at the house in Price, all three dogs sleeping on the thick rag rug at his feet. He'd driven his FJ up from Green River that morning while Wilma Jean, Howie, and Shorty had flown up in her Cessna.

Actually, he mused, they hadn't flown to Price, but had headed from Green River toward Huntington, where they would then criss-cross the section of the Wasatch Plateau where Cy and Christian had gone missing. They would later land in Price, where Bud would meet them at the airport and regroup, depending on what they'd found, if anything.

He'd taken the dogs to the nearby dog park for a bit, then got a couple of tacos at Sherald's Drive-In, then come back to the house, where he'd given the dogs some Barkie Biscuits, pulled some weeds in the flowerbeds, then settled in front of the fireplace, the house still chilly from the storm that had just passed through.

He enjoyed the peace and quiet there, yet felt frustrated from being temporarily out of the loop and not knowing what was going on, though they said they would call him when they got to the airport. He knew he could've gone with them, as his wife's plane would hold four, but his fear of flying held him back.

It had been several hours now, and he knew that the longer they were gone, the higher the odds that they weren't having any luck. He could feel his general optimism beginning to fade as if he were standing on the edge of a dark crevasse looking into blackness, which reminded him of a cup of black coffee, so he got up and put the coffee pot on. No point in fighting things, he figured.

He thought back to when Christian and his grandfather had first come into the cafe several days ago. Cy had mentioned the Grandfathers, as well as the Wanuskewin, whatever that was. He'd intended to look it up on the Internet, but wasn't even sure how to spell it, so it had slipped his mind. Since they'd said they were Cree, it was likely a word from the Cree language—and why was Cy so interested in petroglyphs?

Bud closed his eyes, thinking. Had Cy really crossed the border dressed as a bear? If so, he had a lot of ingenuity, as well as being in good enough shape to cross in what had to be a remote area. Bud knew that a lot of the Canadian-U.S. border wasn't guarded, though he knew there were cameras everywhere.

Cy appeared to be old school, someone used to being self-sufficient, the type of guy who would decide for himself what laws merited following, who felt that land boundaries were a human construct and it was up to individuals as to whether or not to honor them. Cy was Cree, a tribe who had long wandered the countryside in Canada and the northwestern U.S., going wherever they wished as hunter-gatherers, long before borders were established.

He now thought about Cy's wife, Elizabeth, Christian's grandmother. She had cleared up the mystery of the blue feathers, saying Christian was a fancy dancer. But if they were headed to a powwow in Delta, why were they over on the plateau? And why had they come around over Soldier Summit to Price instead of heading straight south, as Delta was southwest of Salt Lake?

Elizabeth had said she was tracking them, looking for something that belonged in a museum. If it had been her grandmother's, why had Cy taken it? She'd said that Cy told her it held some kind of secret.

So far, Bud mused, nothing made sense. Why had Christian hidden his radio in the rocks, wrapped in a pair of mittens? And what was all this about fox hunting? Even Molly had been upset about the fox hunters staying at the B&B. And dire-bear hunting? That was the only part that made any sense at all, Bud thought, since Maddie and Auggie were paleontologists.

But none of this really mattered, Bud decided, other than trying to get the radio back to its owner, which was pretty minor in the grand scheme of things. The rest was all theoretical, kind of like watching a soap opera—lots of interesting loose ends, but nothing really earth-shattering, just a look into the lives of other people, though these were real people, not TV personas. And as far as he could tell, no laws had been broken, so there was nothing he needed to get involved in. The fact that Cy had stolen something from a Canadian museum wasn't in his jurisdiction, and he wasn't even sure if it was true.

What *was* important was the fact that someone had put out an SOS call and was stuck on the plateau, which *was* part of his jurisdiction as Sheriff of Emery County. His inability to make any headway on it was concerning, plus he needed to get back to things in Green River. He knew there was a point when he'd have to give up and continue on without closure.

He thought back to what he was now calling the Dire Bear Cafe, the old Orange Olsen house where Maddie and Auggie were staying. Elizabeth had been certain that Cy and Christian were the ones lost. She swore someone was following them, but why? Was she really able to track Christian's radio with her KrakenSDR? How could she tell it was Christian and not someone else transmitting?

He'd discussed it with Howie, who was adamant that she couldn't possibly tell Christian's signals from anyone else's. But why had she mentioned a birdie? Was she just using a figure of speech? And why were Cy and Christian on the plateau in the first place? There was nothing up there except open country, no towns or ranches, and the roads could be iffy even when dry. Maybe they'd decided to take it as a shortcut on over to the interstate, then go on to Delta.

Bud knew the Wasatch Plateau as well as anyone, except maybe some local hunters, though he hadn't been over it for several years. The main road, the one that Elizabeth had gone up against Bud's advice, was a dirt road that transected the range east-to-west between Ephraim and Orangeville and was generally called the Orangeville-Ephraim Road. It started at Joe's Reservoir, briefly meeting up with Skyline Drive, which traversed the spine of the plateau, then became the Ephraim Road, dropping down to the town of its namesake. The entire drive across the plateau was some 46 miles long.

Once one reached Skyline Drive, built in the 1930s by the Civilian Conservation Corps, you could turn north or south and follow the entire range for over 70 miles, winding along the plateau's summits and ridges, much at elevations above 10,000 feet with high meadows and stands of aspen and conifer, spectacular vistas at every turn. The plateau had eight peaks reaching above 11,000 feet. A number of roads accessed Skyline Drive along its length from Soldier Summit in the north to Interstate 70 in the south.

Bud felt that the plateau was one of the great overlooked places of Utah with its hundreds of high-mountain lakes and reservoirs. It had a quiet beauty to it and was untouched and remote feeling, which is why he suspected it didn't see more people.

Coffee gone, Bud pulled out his harmonica and began fiddling with it, deciding to try a new tune. The old Tennessee Ernie Ford song *Sixteen Tons* came to mind as he thought of Howie's story about listening to the woman who'd lost her family in the Crandall Mine disaster. He once again figured the radio conversation at Scofield Reservoir had to be a prank.

> You load sixteen tons,
> And whatta you get,
> Another day older and deeper in debt.

He then decided he'd prefer learning something a little more upbeat, so started on *Coal Miner's Daughter*, but not really sure of the tune and feeling like he was getting more melancholy by the minute, he decided to instead try that old Jimmie Rodgers classic, the *Yodeling Cowboy*.

He was doing fine until he came to the yodeling part, and not really knowing how to make his harmonica yodel, he gave up and put it back into his pocket, leaning back.

Where were Wilma Jean and the gang? Had something happened?

Just then, his phone rang, and what he heard next seemed to go along with the general mood he'd found himself tumbling into.

"Bud, Shorty here. Wilma Jean's on her way to the hospital in an ambulance, and no, she's fine, but she's with that young guy called Christian. We found him, but he's not in very good shape, and his grandfather's still missing. Can you come pick me and Howie up at the airport?"

"I'll be right there," Bud replied, relieved they were OK, though now concerned about this new turn of affairs.

"Bud," Shorty added. "Christian was mauled by a bear. We need to find his grandfather ASAP."

"A bear?" Bud asked with surprise. "Bear maulings in this area are extremely rare. Black bears are generally leery of people, and we don't have grizzlies."

"I know," Shorty replied. "But Christian said the bear was predatory. We need to get back out there right away, Sheriff."

"Totally agree," Bud said as he grabbed his FJ keys.

"And Bud," Shorty added. "We just talked to a deputy here at the airport, not sure where he was going, but when we told him we'd just found a missing person, he told us a sheepherder had just been mauled out on the plateau. It was in Carbon County, which is why we didn't hear anything about it. He said the guy said it was a bear attack, a really big bear, and he was lucky to get away. There's been rumors going around for several weeks about a large rogue bear out there."

They hung up, and Bud was soon heading out the door, dogs at his heels, wishing he was wandering around aimlessly out in the Big Empty instead of getting ready to go pick up Shorty and Howie and get involved in what could possibly turn into a body recovery.

13

Bud carefully steered the FJ around the muddy spots in the road as they climbed the road above the Dire Bear Cafe. They had just picked Elizabeth up to take her along to help search for Cy. She rode in the front, Shorty in the back, with Lindie by his side. Howie was in the air, flying with Wilma Jean, crisscrossing the area in their aerial search. Bud had left Pierre and Hoppie back at the house with biscuits, bringing only Lindie along.

Elizabeth had insisted on carrying a pack with her, and Bud suspected it held the KrakenSDR and its collapsible antennas, as he'd seen her unscrew them from the rooftop mounts on her pickup.

As if sensing what Bud was thinking, she said, "I have the Kraken. Once we get up out of this valley, we can stop and set the antennas on your roof."

"What good is that going to do us?" Shorty asked. "Doesn't Bud have their radio?"

Elizabeth looked at him with suspicion, then said, "So, I *was* tracking the right signal, eh? And why exactly *do* you have Christian's radio?"

"I found it," Bud replied. "I've been trying to get it back to him."

"And you've been transmitting with it? That's illegal."

"My friend Howie was using it. He has a license," Bud replied. "But how did you know it was Christian's radio? You said something about a birdie."

Elizabeth sighed. "Radio gets too complicated when you try to explain it to non-radio people, but a birdie's a type of spurious signal in your transceiver, a form of interference. It usually sounds like a chirp or warble, so hams call them birdies. The first time I ever heard one I actually thought someone was transmitting bird songs. It's kind of a form of harmonics. For some reason, and nobody can figure out why, Christian's Yaesu always creates a birdie in my transceiver, so I know it's him. It's not supposed to work that way, but it does."

"Interesting," Bud replied. "We wondered how you could tell."

Elizabeth added, "Most hams don't realize that the microphone on their radio has a very distinct signature, a little sound when it unkeys, and even sometimes when it keys up. This sound is unique and can be used to identify the radio, though you need to analyze it visually in an audio spectrum. It's easy to identify a transmitter when you do that, but somehow I'm hearing a birdie with Christian's radio."

Bud asked, "How is your Kraken going to help us now?"

Elizabeth replied, "Christian has a mobile unit in his car, and I know they took it with them when they set out on foot. I'll track it."

"How do you know they took it?" Shorty asked.

"Because they're not going to leave an expensive radio behind, and it's their lifeline. Since Christian's into QRP, the radio is portable."

"What's QRP?" Shorty asked.

"It's operating with very low power, usually lower than five watts. Most radios are 100 watts or more. His is really small, and he has a small portable antenna. It's quite challenging to make contacts, which is why he likes it."

"Does Cy know how to use it?" Shorty asked.

"Of course," Elizabeth answered. "Cy and I are both hams. Christian learned it from us."

"So, you think Cy has the radio and you can track him?" Bud asked. "Won't he run out of power before long?"

"Christian has a small fold-up solar panel that charges the power bank," Elizabeth replied. "He does a lot of SOTA and POTA, where there's no electricity."

"What's that?" Bud asked.

"SOTA is Summits on the Air, and POTA is Parks on the Air. It's contesting. You set up your equipment on a summit or in a national or state park, locate yourself on the Internet, then people contact you on their radios. There's all kinds of certificates one can get. It can be a lot of fun."

"Is there a COTA for Couches on the Air?" Shorty asked. "I could get into that. Or SOTA for Sofas on the Air?"

"You laugh," Elizabeth said, "But there are lots of contests. For example, there's a guy who does LACTOTA for Louis and Clark Trail on the Air."

"Once we get on top of the plateau," Bud said, "I'll stop and we can see if we can rig up the antennas. But you talked to Christian on the phone before we left. How's he doing?"

"He'll be in the hospital for a couple of days, but his wife is coming over from Salt Lake. She'll take him home. He'll be OK."

"How badly was he injured?" Shorty asked.

Elizabeth shook her head. "Fortunately, he was slammed against the truck and only bruised his ribs, but it's very painful."

Bud replied, "I'm confused. Why are bruised ribs fortunate?"

Elizabeth answered, "It's fortunate because he wasn't clawed, like on his face or something. He should heal fast."

Shorty asked, "Did he tell you anything about what happened or why they were up on the plateau?"

"Yes, Cy was hell bent on getting up there for some reason, probably looking for the Grandfathers. Christian told Cy they were going to get stuck, but Cy insisted they keep going. That's Cy for you. He always thinks that he's protected since he's an elder and can do things other people can't. But then, sometimes Christian goes along with it."

"What or who are the Grandfathers?" Bud asked.

"I can't talk about that," Elizabeth replied. "You'll have to ask Cy."

"Did he say how they got into it with a bear?" Shorty asked.

"Yes. They got stuck, so they decided to abandon the Silverado and walk back. It was getting dark, and Christian said he could hear something following them. He immediately decided they should get back to the truck, so they turned around and tried to cut sideways away from whatever it was, and just as they made it back, it attacked. They both jumped into the car, but the bear slammed Christian as he jumped in. It was dark, so he couldn't see it really well."

She continued. "Cy called out an SOS several times on the radio. By morning, since no one showed up, Cy figured he had to do something, so he started walking back. Christian was in a lot of pain so couldn't go, and he tried to stop him, but Cy wouldn't listen. That's the last anyone has seen of him, and you know the rest of the story. Your bunch found Christian and flew him to Price. But we have to find Cy. He's on heart medication and must be running low. And that bear…"

"We'll find him, Elizabeth," Bud replied. "My wife and friend are flying around looking as we speak, and the local SAR group is gearing up. We're almost to where the Silverado's stuck, and we can regroup from there and decide what to do next."

"He's tough," she added. "But not as tough as he'd like one to think. He *is* getting old."

"How old is he?" Shorty asked.

"Eighty-two," she replied. "I'm a lot younger, just 75. But Sheriff…"

Her voice trailed off until Bud finally said, "Go ahead, Elizabeth."

"I don't want to cause suspicion where it's not merited," she said, again stopping, then finally adding, "But that person, the one back at what you guys call the Dire Bear Cafe? Well, she said something that made me really wonder what they're up to. I don't know, maybe I'm reading something into it, and she and Auggie were both very good to me, feeding me and putting me up for the night, but…"

"Spill the beans," Shorty said. "You're talking to the sheriff."

Giving Shorty an exasperated look, she continued.

"OK, they started talking about some bones they'd just found, some dire-bear bones, and she said she thinks they're well enough preserved that they can extract some DNA and maybe sequence the genetics to where they could even recreate the species. Something about there being enough protein."

"That's the dream of every paleontologist," Shorty replied. "There's a guy at a museum in Montana who's been trying to sequence dinosaur DNA for years. It's never going to happen."

"Shorty's a professional geologist, Elizabeth, just so you know," Bud added. "Though he's retired."

"I didn't know that," she said. "That's all fine and dandy, but it's what else she said that made me wonder. It was like she'd just realized I was listening, because she told Auggie to not mention the bear. And Auggie said, 'You mean the one that's made it too dangerous to camp so now we have to rent this place? The one that's made you start carrying a gun? The one that's making me wish I'd never been a part of this project? The one that if I didn't have a family to feed, I'd be long gone? The one who attacked that poor sheepherder?' He sounded really angry. She kept saying, 'Focus, Auggie, focus,' then said she'd saved the sheepherder, hadn't she, and then she left. I thought she'd maybe gone for a walk down by the lake, but then I saw her sitting in their van. She didn't come back in until dark. She went to her room and he went to his, and as far as I know, neither of them spoke to each other the rest of the night."

"Did they know about Christian at that point?" Bud asked.

"No, I didn't find out until the next morning, and by then they were both up at that cave, so as far as I know, they're still unaware of it."

They had now topped out and were approaching a long grassy meadow surrounded by aspen trees.

Bud pulled the FJ over onto a flat spot as he said, "I'm wondering how Maddie could have possibly known about the sheepherder getting mauled. They're clear over here out of the loop, and it basically just happened. And what did she mean when she said she'd saved the sheepherder? They were miles away."

He paused, then asked, "Shorty, you think there could be a dire bear running around on the plateau? Or maybe something related to one?"

"Shades of *Jurassic Park?*" Shorty asked, letting Lindie out. "And no, it's not possible, Bud. Science hasn't cracked that nut yet."

"Your dog says there's something over in the trees," Elizabeth said, pointing at Lindie, who was on high alert, ears forward.

As Lindie started growling, Bud quickly got her back into the FJ.

"It's Cy!" Elizabeth said as the old man stumbled from the aspens.

"That's the quickest rescue I've ever been on," Shorty said as they rushed to Cy's side.

"He doesn't look too bad for the wear," Bud replied as they helped him to the FJ. "I'll get on the horn to Wilma Jean. She can land on the road here and take him to the hospital to get checked out. We can go get their Silverado unstuck and then go home, case closed."

They eased Cy into the front seat, and before long, into Wilma Jean's Cessna in the back seat next to Howie, Elizabeth in the front.

Bud watched as the plane bumped down the dirt road, quickly taking to the air. Wilma Jean and Howie would take Cy and Elizabeth to the airport, where an ambulance would meet them, though Bud suspected Cy's stay there would be brief. He and Howie would retrieve the Silverado and then hopefully go on home.

14

"Are you sure there can't be dire bears in these woods?" Bud asked, steering the FJ around a deep pothole as they made their way from the Orange Olsen house to the top of the plateau.

It was the next day, and Wilma Jean and Howie had flown back to Green River with the two dogs, Lindie staying behind with Bud and Shorty at the Price house. They had decided to stay in case Elizabeth and Cy needed help, plus they would get Christian's car.

"There are dire bears here only if we use a time machine," Shorty replied. "One that goes back 10,000 years. But without that, there are only a few blackies up here."

"*Rogue* blackies," Bud said warily. "And what about the bear that injured the sheepherder over in Carbon County? But here's Christian's Silverado, at the exact coordinates Wilma Jean gave us. Now if we can only get it out of the mud pit they seem to have dug it into."

Bud parked the FJ near the pickup, which was up to its axles in mud.

"At least things appear to have dried out," Shorty said. "Cy gave you the keys?"

"He did. Hopefully they didn't drain the battery trying to get it unstuck."

As Bud pulled a tow strap from the back of the FJ, Lindie started to jump out, but he told her to stay.

"We don't need dogs chasing bears," Bud added. "Though I doubt very much if one's around."

"Better safe than sorry," Shorty said, glancing toward the nearby woods as he walked around the Silverado. "But come take a look, Sheriff. It appears someone tried to break into the pickup—actually, *did* break in from the looks of this window."

They stood looking at the shattered glass of the rear passenger window, the back club cab door hanging open.

Bud said, "Cy said someone had been following them. But whoever did this only broke one window so they could open the door from inside. Not the work of a bear. And it appears they rummaged through Cy and Christian's stuff, the way it's strewn all over."

"Are you sure it wasn't that bear they said was stalking them, Bud?" Shorty asked. "It broke the window and went through everything."

"Only one problem with that theory, Shorty," Bud replied as they began picking up everything. "Bears can't open vehicle doors. And look at their cooler—it's been opened. I think a person did this. A bear would destroy the cooler to get into it, not neatly open the lid. And the glove box is also open."

"Look at this, Sheriff," Shorty said, pointing to a trail of blue feathers that led into the nearby aspens. "Looks like some kind of bluebird was kidnapped, a really *big* bluebird."

Bud laughed. "That's Christian's fancy-dance outfit, or what's left of it. But why would someone drag that off? Who would want it?"

"Maybe the bear visited after the human broke in and then dragged the costume off," Shorty replied. "Maybe it fancies itself a fancy dancer. But we need to get this vehicle out of here."

They soon had the Silverado attached to the tow strap, and Bud slowly began backing, pulling it from the mud, as Shorty drove, watching to make sure the strap didn't break.

The Silverado finally back on the road, Shorty said, "That's a relief." He began kicking dried mud from the wheels.

"We can head back now," Bud said, putting the tow strap away.

"Except it's almost out of gas," Shorty said. "I'm not sure we can get back with it on empty."

"I have an extra can on my bumper, Shorty. I always carry extra gas and water."

"Always prepared," Shorty replied. "Let's have a cup of coffee before we head back. You have your coffee kit with you, don't you?"

"Just like gas and water, we can't survive without coffee," Bud grinned, turning off the FJ. "Besides, I need to look around a bit more."

Bud started his little camp stove, then looked all around where the truck had been as they waited for the water to boil. Before long, they were savoring cups of hot coffee.

"Man, this stuff's stout," Shorty said. "You need some of that freeze-dried ice cream like NASA sends up with the astronauts."

They sat in silence, savoring the hot drink as the sun poked through the aspens, the golden leaves turning in the breeze.

"We're seeing the end of the season, Shorty," Bud said. "It's nice we could get up here, even if just for a few hours. This place is really nice in the autumn. I need to come up here with my camera."

Shorty was silent for a moment, then began looking around. "Bud, I suddenly have the feeling we're being watched. Do you feel anything?"

"No. It's probably from all the bear talk. Let's finish our coffee and head out."

"Bud, we've talked about bears when out in the woods before— remember when we were up in Tombstone Territorial Park in the Yukon, where there are lots of grizzlies? It didn't feel like this. You don't feel something kind of ominous?"

Bud shook his head no, adding, "Lindie's asleep in the FJ. If there were something around, she'd be on high alert."

"Now I'm getting goosebumps," Shorty added. "There has to be something around. My intuition is pretty well developed after living in the Yukon for so long."

Bud sipped his coffee. "Did you know that goosebumps are

caused by the tiny muscles around your hair follicles expanding? I read that in a book somewhere. It's a leftover survival thing for when we lived with predators. It makes us look larger and more intimidating, kind of like the hackles on a dog."

Shorty, now standing, said, "We need to head out. Don't you feel even a little bit nervous?"

Bud also stood. "Well now that you mention it, maybe a little bit, but I think it's from you talking about it, since fear's contagious. But Shorty, if those guys were being stalked by a bear, wouldn't you think we'd see a track or two, especially given all the mud?"

"You didn't find any tracks?"

"No, and I walked all around. I did find an extra set of human tracks, though. Three distinct types of boots, two which I assume were Christian and Cy's, but a third that was different, a hiking boot, and smaller. The only problem is, the mud made it hard to get a good definition of what kind of boots or what size. If a bear was following them, it left before they got back to the Silverado."

"Maybe it stole someone's shoes," Shorty joked. "But wasn't Christian slammed against the truck? He said it was a bear."

"Have you ever seen a bear body slam anyone? They use their claws and teeth, Shorty. But you know, when I first met those two, they were being followed by some guys who said they were fox hunters. I'm wondering if there's not some connection."

"Why would they be following them if they were hunting foxes?"

"Good question. But Lindie's awake now and acts like she sees something in the trees. Look how she's holding her ears forward. We need to put some gas in the truck and head out."

Shorty replied, "Bud, my senses are on super high alert. Let's go on down the road a couple of miles to where we found Cy and put gas in there. It feels safer. I swear, there's something out here watching us."

"Shorty, I have the upmost respect for your intuition after the years you spent wandering around in the wilds. I'll follow you in case you run out of gas. Stop a few miles down the road."

"Done," Shorty replied, getting into the Silverado and starting it.

They were soon gone, neither of them aware of the large shadow that stepped from the trees, watching their departure. It turned, and several blue feathers that had been caught in its fur were lifted by the breeze, drifting into the nearby bushes, where they would rest through the long winter, forgotten.

15

"Cy, did Elizabeth go back to Salt Lake with Christian?" Bud asked.

He and Shorty sat in camp chairs in the back yard of the house in Price, while Cy, who looked worn and tired, leaned back in a somewhat tattered chaise lounge chair that Wilma Jean had bought on the local swap.

"They're long gone," he moaned. "They totally abandoned me—Elizabeth did, anyway. I'm glad you guys stuck around to get me out of the hospital."

"I thought they needed her to watch the great-grandkids," Shorty replied. "But what about her pickup?"

"It's still up at the Dire Bear Cafe," Bud replied. "Elizabeth left the keys with me when she flew out with you and Wilma Jean, and it's still sitting there."

"I need somebody to help me go get it," Cy said.

"We'll take care of it," Bud said. "As soon as you're feeling good enough to drive it. Elizabeth and Christian both want you to stay here for a few days and get your strength back, and we all think it's a good idea. We've stocked up the fridge, and our good friends Hattie and Tex are going to check in on you and see if you need anything. We need to get back to Green River, but we'll be back in a day or two and take you out to get your truck."

"I need those keys," Cy said. You need to leave them with me. I feel fine. I have things to do."

"They're not going to take you out there," Bud said. "They have strict orders not to. Look, you were released from the hospital pretty quickly, but they had you on a drip for a reason—you were dehydrated. There's lots of Gatorade and cold drinks in the fridge, so be sure and drink them. We'll be back and take you to your truck."

"It's Elizabeth's," Cy replied. "I'm surprised she's going to let me drive it. Are you sure she knows? She never lets me drive it. But did you buy stuff to make bologna sandwiches? I eat lots of bologna sandwiches."

"That explains a few things," Shorty laughed. "Are you back on your heart meds? Are you going back to Saskatchewan?"

Cy leaned back, sighing. "I quit taking those years ago, though Elizabeth doesn't know. I feel better without them. But I'm afraid to go back to Swift Current. I've angered the bear gods."

"The bear guards?" Shorty asked.

"No, the gods. The bear gods," Cy replied with irritation.

"How did you do that?" Bud asked patiently.

"By pretending I was a bear. I bought a ghillie suit off eBay, you know, the ones the military uses to make them look like bushes. Then I painted my face dark brown and walked across the border. I hid the suit under some rocks and can use it to get back in if I need to. The bear gods decided it was sacrilege and I was mocking them, and now Christian has paid the price."

"Do you really believe that, Cy?" Bud asked.

"Look, I'm a Cree elder, and you're a sheriff. As sheriff, part of your job is to be prepared. As an elder, part of my job is to carry on the old traditions and stories."

"So, you kinda sorta believe you've angered the gods?" Bud asked.

"Maybe not one-hundred percent."

"Did you ever hear of Old Ephraim?" Shorty asked.

"No. Sounds like someone from the Bible."

Shorty continued. "The name may be. Ephraim is what early trappers and settlers called grizzly bears. Grizzlies used to have an extensive range that once extended from California to central Mexico and to the prairies of the midwestern states. They now have only about two percent of that territory, mostly in deep wilderness. Stockmen hate grizzlies and were mostly responsible for decimating them. Old Ephraim was one of the last grizzlies in Utah. He's become a kind of folk hero."

"How can a bear be a hero?" Cy asked.

"Old Ephraim was famous for his intelligence and ability to outwit humans. Grizzlies are smart, maybe even smarter than most primates. They've been known to cover their own tracks and to conceal themselves with trees and rocks when hunting. Old Eph lived in Logan Canyon, not far from Utah State University, where his skull is now on display."

"So, I assume someone killed him?"

"Yes, a sheepherder named Frank Clark ran his sheep in the canyon, and Old Eph had a taste for them. It took Clark over a decade to even get a good look at Old Ephraim, much less a clear shot at him, but he eventually killed him in 1923. There's a stone monument to Old Eph up in Logan Canyon where Clark buried him. It has a poem on it:

> Old Ephraim, Old Ephraim, your deeds were so
> wrong,
> Yet we build you this marker and sing you this song.
> To the king of the forest so mighty and tall,
> We salute you, Old Ephraim, the king of them all.

Bud added, "Clark later said he regretted killing him."

"How did he know it was the same bear through all that time?" Cy asked.

Shorty replied, "By his tracks. He had three toes. His fame came from his ability to outwit traps. He's become a legend."

"So, am I following when you think maybe there's a grizz on the plateau? One that stalked us and then attacked Christian?"

"It's possible, Cy. Grizzlies roam in Idaho, Wyoming, and Montana and have even been sighted in northwest Colorado. It's not a stretch to think one could be on the plateau, especially given how remote it is."

"Whatever it was, it was scary," Cy replied thoughtfully. "And I swear it was wearing a necklace, actually, it looked like a double necklace. We were doing real good until Christian put it in the rhubarb."

"Drove into the ditch?" Bud asked.

"Exactly."

Bud thought for awhile, then said, "Cy, I do think you were being followed, but by something much worse than a bear."

"Worse? What could be worse?"

"A human. Or maybe several."

"It definitely was a bear. A *big* bear."

"You actually saw it?" Shorty asked.

"I saw something."

"You saw it in the dark," Shorty added. "Right?"

"Cy, there was plenty of mud when we got Christian's truck out. Dried mud. Lots of tracks, but no bear tracks."

"Maybe it was like Old Ephraim, elusive," Cy replied.

"Or human," Bud said. "Maybe someone looking for something you and Christian supposedly have."

Cy sighed. "So, Elizabeth told you all about her museum treasure, I gather."

"All she said was that you had something that belonged in a museum, and she wanted it back."

"She donated it, well, the museum had it on loan. I admit it, I took it from the museum—borrowed it, that is. As an elder and one of the docents there, I can mess around with stuff when I want."

"Where is this so-called museum piece?" Bud asked. "There's nothing in your car, just your clothes and such, which were strewn all over the place, like someone looking for something."

"They won't find it there," Cy replied. "Christian hid it."

"Can you tell us what it is so we'll know if we see it?" Shorty asked.

"Nope. Can't talk about it. Can't talk about the Grandfathers."

"It has to do with the Grandfathers?"

"Can't say. Where are the pickup keys? You can't take them. You'll get in trouble for grand theft auto, Sheriff. I'll turn you in. How's it gonna look when the sheriff has a rap sheet?"

"About how entering the U.S. illegally might look," Shorty replied.

Cy blanched. "I'm perfectly legal. I have a valid driver's license. I pay my taxes, too—paid them several years ago."

"You need a passport," Shorty replied.

"Shorty's a dual citizen, Cy. He knows the rules," Bud added.

Shorty nodded. "Elizabeth should take you back to Canada."

"Will they let me back in?" Cy asked.

Shorty replied, "It's illegal to leave someone with no home country, so they will."

"That's a relief," Cy replied. "They let me in last time, too. Where's Christian's pickup?"

"We left it at a shop to get the window fixed," Bud replied. "We figured you'd be needing it to get back to Salt Lake."

"That was awfully nice of you," Cy replied. "Now I'll have two vehicles to drive."

"Christian asked us to," Bud replied. "He's going to ride the train back here and get it when it's ready."

Cy perked up. "He's doing OK?"

"He seems fine, just bruised. But we need to get back to Green River. You just stay put here, rest up, and we'll be back to get your pickup."

"I'm glad I took Christian's mobile radio so nothing happened to it. Where is it, by the way?"

"Your pack's in the kitchen," Bud said. "Along with your clothes from the car."

With that, they went inside the house, Bud leaving the pickup keys on the kitchen counter. As they left, Lindie jumped into the FJ as Shorty said, "Do you think he'll wait for us to go get it?"

"Not a chance," Bud replied. "And I'll bet you anything he's back up on the plateau before you can say *grandfathers*. I don't know what he's looking for, but anything that would spur him to cross the border illegally has to be super important in his mind. And I don't think it's a pair of mittens."

"And you can add one more thing to that bet, Sheriff," Shorty added.

"Oh?"

"Another search and rescue on the plateau."

"Wouldn't surprise me one bit."

With that, they happily headed back to Green River.

16

Bud sat in his office, feet up on a nearby chair, trying not to doze off, still tired from running around with Shorty and Howie the previous couple of days. It was nice to be back in Green River, where nothing much ever happened.

He knew he should get out to the farm soon and check with Kale to see how the harvest was going, though he knew he wasn't really needed. It was more of a way to show his support through what was typically a busy time of year, though Kale and his workers usually had everything under control.

He wondered if Cy had stayed put like he'd been advised, though something told him the old guy was probably on his way at that very moment to get Elizabeth's pickup.

Oh well, he mused, Cy had a few years on him and surely knew his own capabilities, though he sure wished he knew what the mysterious museum object was. He'd even done a quick Internet search on *Canada museum piece stolen* but hadn't found anything of interest, other than something called the 1972 Skylight Caper, where thieves entered the Montreal Museum of Fine Arts through a skylight and stole paintings by Rembrandt, Rubens, and Delacroix.

He'd heard of Rembrandt and Rubens, but not Delacroix, and he soon lost interest, wondering what the special down at the Melon Rind was for the day—it was Wednesday, so it was probably roast beef over homemade Texas toast smothered with thick brown gravy.

Just then, with no warning, his office door swung open with a crash, and a short woman wearing blue Bermuda shorts and carrying a postal bag pushed a young guy in front of her, the guy's arm skewed behind his back. The young guy was wearing cargo pants and a t-shirt with the word *SEEN* in outline bubble form with bright colors.

"Sheriff, I caught this hoodlum red-handed spray painting a train car," the woman said in disgust. "Arrest him for vandalism."

"It's called art, not vandalism," the young guy said, pulling free.

Bud groaned. "Wanda, I've told you a million times to call me and not try to arrest someone yourself. You're going to get yourself in trouble one of these days."

Wanda replied, "I can't just ignore someone committing a crime. By the time I reported it, he'd be long gone."

The young guy said, "I can't leave. The trains here don't stop. They don't even slow down."

"Is that how you got here?" Wanda asked.

"I ride the trains. I live the graff life. I'm what's called a hobo artist. I do edgy and gallery-quality art, which you interrupted."

The young guy, seeming to suddenly realize where he was, added, "And Sheriff, I have permission to be here—from the railroad."

Wanda guffawed. "Not likely, buckaroo. Look, you may think of yourself as an artist, but if you're going to do criminal things, you're a criminal. Arrest him, Bud."

Bud replied, "Wanda, you go on back to work, I've got this. I'll call the railroad and see if he's telling the truth, and if not, we'll decide from there. No more citizen's arrests."

"He should at least do some community service," Wanda said, reluctantly going back out the door.

"Have a seat, young man," Bud said, pointing to the chair he'd just had his feet on. "What's your name? Can I see your ID?"

The guy reluctantly pulled a driver's license from his back pocket, handing it to Bud, who read, "Chance Waters from Detroit, Michigan. Is this your current address?"

The guy looked at the floor, saying, "That's my mom's address, but I stay there sometimes. I don't actually have a permanent address because I'm a hobo. I ride the rails, and I decorate the trains. But who was that woman, anyway? She's scary, and being from Detroit, I've seen it all."

Bud replied, "That's Wanda, our postal carrier. Have you been arrested before?"

A long pause, then Chance said, "Man, I'd hate to meet your post-master. I've maybe been arrested a couple of times, but that was before I knew not to paint over the numbers, Sheriff. I don't do that now, and when the railroad guys see me, they don't pay me no mind, because they know I'm gonna just decorate the trains for the American public. They enjoy seeing it."

He continued. "I started when I was just a kid, using ketchup from a squirt bottle on toast. I discovered I had artistic talent. I started tagging things with flying saucers and clowns and progressed from there, doing things like dogs and bubble letters. I eventually discovered trains and realized I could make art that would travel the whole country for people to see, a traveling art show."

"So you primarily do trains and not buildings and walls and such?" Bud asked.

"I'm not like a regular tag artist, Sheriff. I do *only* trains—stuff like fish and mountains and stuff like that. I used to do stupid stuff, but I've matured as an artist. Sometimes I even put stuff like polar bears and penguins on the trains. I figure my art stuff might be the only wildlife some little kid in the inner city will ever see."

"And the train yard guys don't object to this?" Bud asked.

"Once in a while," Chance replied. "But the ones who know me leave me alone. They like my graph art—it makes their days a little brighter, and I've even had a couple tell me it makes it easier for them to spot certain cars when they're moving things around."

"How would that work?" Bud asked.

"Like, if I put an eagle on a car, then that's pretty distinct and it helps them out. I even painted an auto rack to look like a grasshopper once, took tons of cans. The train guys said it looked amazing. But yeah, some so-called graph artists just put junk on the trains, and the train guys don't like that. But in general, the carriers don't care. Fresh freight cars are a boring thing, Sheriff. Graffiti is a rite of passage for a rail car. Car number and information have to be visible, any respectable graffiti artist knows this, and units and passenger trains are off limits. The rules are don't interfere with railroad operations, and be a ghost."

"What's a unit?" Bud asked. "And what's your artist name? How will I know if it was you who painted something?"

"A unit's an engine. I go by Blue Moon, as in once in a blue moon, you know, that's how often you take a chance. Some of us are respected artists, like the guy on my t-shirt here, *SEEN*. He's really well-known and does beautiful work. He's called the Godfather of Graffiti and is famous for his bright colors and cartoon characters."

"Interesting," Bud said, watching out the window as Howie walked across the street from his drive-in. "How do you support yourself doing this?"

Chance replied, "I kind of don't, though sometimes I'll get a job doing a mural for someone. I can live a long time on that kind of thing, but sometimes I'll do chores for food, like help at a cafe."

Bud stood. "My good friend the town mayor is about to come in, and he owns the drive-in across the street. I'm going to buy you a burger, but I don't want to hear or see anything to do with graffiti. Deal?"

"You bet!" Chance replied enthusiastically. "Is there a hobo jungle around here where I can camp until a train comes through? One that slows down, I mean."

Bud replied, "Just head down to the river and camp on any of the beaches. And as for tagging trains, I would advise you not to. Wanda's sort of a self-appointed deputy, and if she sees you, she'll be dragging you back in here, and I'll have to explain why I didn't arrest you. Let's just lay off that for now."

"Done," Chance replied as Howie walked in the door. "I'll lay low and be like a normal hobo."

"You know," Bud said thoughtfully. "I have a soft spot for hobos. Don't take advantage of it."

"I won't," Chance replied. "Did you used to be one?"

"No, but my Uncle Junior was."

"Did he get hit by a train or something?"

"No, fortunately not. He got married and runs around in an RV now instead of riding the rails. He and his wife LouAnn are somewhere out there in an RV as we speak—last I heard up in Oregon— wild and free."

"That's awesome. I'm gonna do that when I can't hop freights anymore."

Howie said, "Morning sheriff. Am I interrupting something? You thinking about becoming a hobo?"

"Howie, this is Chance. He's a hobo artist. Chance, Mayor Howie."

"You mean he does graffiti?" Howie asked. "Can you do murals? I've been thinking about getting one on the drive-in. And now that you mention it, it might be kind of fun to have a few painted on the windows around town for Melon Days."

Bud replied, "Well, I didn't mention it, but I think that would be a good idea. I'm going to buy Chance a burger at your place, Howie, so I guess you guys can talk about it over there. I need to get back to work."

"I'll donate his lunch as a thank you to Emery County law enforcement for furthering the town's artistic interests," Howie said.

"I need the sheriff's permission to do any art around here," Chance said, looking at Bud.

"You have my permission, as long as it's under the mayor's umbrella."

"Let's go get lunch and talk," Howie said, he and Chance walking out the door as Bud added, "Watch out for Wanda, and stay out of trouble."

17

Bud wasn't really sure why he'd told Howie he needed to get back to work, because there really wasn't much to do, but he felt like he just needed some time to himself, some time to try to process the last several days of activity.

He opened his *Outdoor Photography* magazine but soon closed it again, as he couldn't seem to concentrate. Next, he booted up his computer and keyed in *Bermuda shorts,* thinking of how Wanda always wore them.

> *In 1914, native Bermudian and shop owner Nathaniel Coxon encouraged his employees to wear short pants to alleviate the summer heat. The British Army, stationed in Bermuda during World War I, adopted the shorts for wear in tropical and desert climates.*

He shut his laptop, quickly losing interest, leaning back and closing his eyes. Maybe what he needed was a nap, he mused, as that's when he seemed to do his best thinking.

Still awake after a few minutes, he decided he just needed to find something of interest. Maybe he should go back out to the farm where he could help with the harvest. He knew Kale could find something for him to do, though he probably wouldn't get home till late.

No, he needed time to himself, time to think. He wondered if Elizabeth was now back in Salt Lake and if Cy was still at the house in Price.

He thought again of the mysterious museum piece—what could it possibly be, and what kind of special message did it hold, and who exactly was looking for it? Were the fox hunters really fox hunting, or were they hunting something else? Maybe he should get up to the museum in Price and meet with the guy Howie had talked to on the radio who'd said he'd been part of the fox-hunting group.

He now thought back to Tusher Canyon and finding Christian's radio. From what Cy had said, it sounded like Christian had definitely meant to hide the radio, but from who and why? And when had he intended to retrieve it?

His thoughts now went to Maddie and Auggie and their supposed excavation in the cave at Joe's Valley. What had Auggie meant when Elizabeth had overheard him chewing Maddie out over some kind of bear, saying it had made things so dangerous they could no longer camp? Was this related to Shorty's premonitions when they were retrieving Christian's truck up on the plateau? And how could a bear possibly be wearing a necklace, like Cy claimed he saw—or maybe even a double necklace? Was it somehow related to the sheepherder who'd been mauled? He knew bears had large ranges and could move fast—was it possible it was the same bear Cy saw near Joe's Valley, assuming he'd actually seen one?

He again opened his laptop, searching on the word *Pleistocene*.

The Pleistocene Epoch is often referred to as the Ice Age and occurred from 2.6 million to approximately 10,000 years ago. It was characterized by repeated glaciations and major climate changes, leading to the extinction of various megafauna, including mammoths, mastodons, giant sloths, dire bears, and saber-toothed cats.

A rich and extensive fossil record verifies that it was a time of dramatic climate change, significant biodiversity loss, and the emergence and expan-

sion of early humans. Animals that survived the epoch and still exist
include moose, elk, bison, cheetahs, muskoxen, caribou, wolves, and brown
bears. The end of the Pleistocene was marked by rising temperatures, sea-
level rise, and melting glaciers, ushering in the next epoch, the Holocene.

He thought back to accounts he'd read from early explorers in the
Americas, people like Lewis and Clark, and their descriptions of the
richness of the landscape and its numerous inhabitants, of streams
teeming with fish and of meadows with large herds of elk and deer,
and he suddenly felt a sense of nostalgia for something he'd never
known—a world with no cities, no vehicles, no roads, no airplanes, a
world with only plants and animals and incredible views of the
night sky.

He stood and walked over to the large map on the wall on the far
end of his small office, a map of Emory County, his jurisdiction. He
knew parts of the area like the back of his hand, but other parts
seemed mysterious—and with the exception of the portions in the
deep canyons, most of that mystery was in the Wasatch Plateau. It
being mostly unpopulated, he seldom had reason to go there.

He'd tried looking up the name *Wasatch* once to see where it
came from, but never got a clear answer. One historian said it was a
Ute Indian word meaning *mountain pass* or *low pass over high range*
and another said it was a Shoshoni leader's name and meant *blue
heron.* In any case, it was also the name of the impressive mountain
range that bordered Salt Lake City, and Bud knew people often
confused that range with the plateau.

Sitting back down, he suddenly felt like he wanted nothing more
than to go home to the comfort of the bungalow and the boys.

He'd felt this way before, but never while sitting in his office, it
was something that was typically associated with being in wild
places, like the time he was far from civilization on the Top of the
World Highway in the Yukon.

He tried to analyze the feeling, work his way through it, when it
dawned on him that he was feeling the effects of Shorty's nervous-
ness up on the plateau when they were getting Christian's Silverado.

Shorty was a geologist, a scientist, and one of the most pragmatic people Bud knew, a man who had lived for months in a tent in the Yukon wilds while field mapping, never worrying about bears, and yet he'd been truly fearful and wanting to get off the plateau.

What had prompted the feeling? Bud admitted to sensing it himself, though not as strong as Shorty. He'd been around plenty of black bears and never felt that way, though he suspected it had to do with the mauled sheepherder. And now, the unknown quality of it all had followed him down to Green River, making him crave the security of home and his dogs.

He thought again of Maddie and Auggie and what Elizabeth had told him. Was some kind of experiment being conducted on the plateau, something to do with bears, maybe even dire bears? Shorty had said bringing one back to life was impossible, but maybe they'd conjured up something, a similar type of bear. Yet they'd seemed straightforward when Bud and Shorty had talked to them, nothing unusual in their behavior, just two typical science types.

It was too early to go home, Bud decided, taking his harmonica from his pocket, but instead of playing it, he fiddled with it, running his thumb up and down the reeds.

He still felt unsettled, but wasn't sure what to do with the feeling except to try to wear it out and hope it would go away. He knew dinner with Wilma Jean would probably do the trick, if he could just hold out that long.

Finally, something dawned on him—he still had the mittens in his safe, the ones that had been wrapped around Christian's radio. He got up and took them out, carefully examining them, rubbing the soft wool with his fingertips.

He didn't know much about textiles or knitting, but anyone could see that they were high quality, the dark-purple wool worn to a smooth sheen. And what wool it was! It had a soft luxurious feel, the strands having a slight waviness with a delicate almost fuzzy texture, light seeming to actually reflect off the wool, creating a subtle shine.

He was again put off by the roughness of the yellow lightning-bolt pattern going across the middle of each mitten and wrapping around the back. It was a shame, he thought, for the mittens would easily win grand-champion in a county fair if it wasn't for the bolts. Maybe a second person had knitted that part, someone who was just learning. Whoever knitted the mittens themselves seemed to have a high pride of craftsmanship, but the bolts were almost like something a child would knit.

He again ran his fingers over the zigzags. The knitting was rough, with tiny bumps like little nodules. He held them up to the light from the window and could now see that they almost looked like needle-point with an assortment of little round periods and dashes.

He suddenly sat straight up! Could this be the museum piece everyone was looking for? It seemed improbable, but the dots and dashes definitely seemed like some kind of code.

Stunned, he took out a piece of paper and began carefully writing down each dot and dash, starting on the front of the right-hand mitten and going around the back, then doing the same with the left-hand one. Wide spaces separated each combination of dots and dashes, so he substituted slash marks, figuring the spaces were the knitter's way of separating words.

Finished, he examined what he'd copied:

..-. .-. --. - -. / .--. .-. .. .. -. -.-. .... / . .-.. .-- .. --.. / -.-. --- ..- ... .. -. / . .-.. .. --.. / -.--
.-. / .-- -. .-.- / .- - / -... .-.-.- / .-.. -.- / -. .... -..

It made no sense to him, but he suspected he'd just copied some kind of secret message, a message knit in Morse code.

He'd talk to Howie at some point, but for now, inexplicably feeling much better, he put the mittens back in the safe, stuck the paper with the code in his pocket, and went on home.

18

It was the next morning, and Bud sat in the Melon Rind Cafe, watching customers come and go as he sipped a cup of hot coffee.

He was wondering where Howie was, thinking he'd give him a call soon to see if he could decipher the code he'd copied from the mittens the previous day.

Just then, Howie came in the door, followed by Chance, both looking excited. Howie scooted into the booth across from Bud, motioning for Chance to sit next to him.

"Bud, can you spell E-M-E?" Howie asked.

"Is it spelled like it sounds, E-M-E?" Bud asked.

"You got it!" Howie replied.

"And I think I can also spell it backwards. But what does it mean?" Bud asked.

"Earth-Moon-Earth. It means we're going to do a moon bounce, Sheriff."

"And after that, Howie's going to show me how to turn a hotdog into a radio receiver," Chance said. "Sheriff, this is way more fun than trains."

"How are you going to do a moon bounce?" Bud asked. "And what exactly are you going to bounce off the moon?"

"I've been talking with that guy up at the museum in Price, Bud, and he has the equipment to do this. He sent me a photo of his radio shack. It looks like the radio room on a 1930s steamship."

"So, you're planning on going up to Price? Could you check on Cy while you're there?"

"Sure, we can do that," Howie replied. "But I was hoping you'd come along."

"Howie, can you track a radio collar with a ham radio?"

"I'm not sure, Sheriff. Probably, if it's the right frequency. Why do you ask?"

"I've been thinking of what Cy said about the bear they saw. He said it was wearing a necklace. I'm thinking it was a radio collar."

"I thought you decided it couldn't have been a bear because of no tracks."

"That part's a mystery, but he was certain he saw a bear, and a necklace could be a collar. If there is something up there, maybe we can track it."

"We'd need to be up on the plateau, of course."

"Of course," Bud replied.

Howie added, "Jim, the education coordinator at the museum, has offered to take us up onto Ford Ridge where their club repeater is. He needs to do some maintenance on it. That's after we do the moon bounce."

"Tell him what a moon bounce is, Mayor," Chance said.

Howie continued. "My uncle liked to do moon bounces when the conditions were right. I remember him telling me to say something to the moon over the radio, so I said, 'Hello, Moon,' and a couple of seconds later I heard my own voice saying, 'Hello, Moon.' He'd bounced the signal off the moon and back to us. It's called EME, or Earth-Moon-Earth communications."

"Isn't that cool?" Chance said, looking at Howie in admiration.

Howie added, "Radio signals travel the speed of light, so you can gauge how long it'll take, as the speed of light is 186,000 miles per second. The moon's 238,855 miles from the earth, which is about 30 Earths away, so it takes about two and one-half seconds to hit the moon and bounce back, depending on which part of the moon you hit. It works best when the moon's in apogee and overhead, and you need a clear line of sight to the moon."

"If you look outside," Chance said, "You'll see the moon's up. It should work really well, if we can get up to Price."

"So what's the point, other than just for fun?" Bud asked.

"It allows you to make contacts over vast distances, like thousands of miles, without relying on traditional propagation methods, like ionospheric reflection. Plus it's a challenge, as you have to deal with things like polarization of the signal and Doppler effect. It's a lot of fun, Bud. Talking to someone on the other side of the planet is pretty cool, especially if the moon's helping."

"It's called radio magic," Chance said. "But we need to get going."

Now thinking of the Morse code note in his pocket, Bud said, "Fellows, I'm going to have to beg off this one. I've been gone too much lately, and I need some time to tend to things around here. But check on Cy for me, and Howie, see if you can decode this message."

He handed Howie the note, adding, "You do remember your Morse code, right? I put slashes where I thought the word ended."

"You never forget Morse code once you know it," Howie replied. "It's the original binary code with two basic elements, a dot and a dash. Each letter is made up of combinations of dots and dashes. I can decode it right now for you, Sheriff, if you have something to write on."

Bud handed Howie a pen, and Howie began writing on a napkin:

FRGTN PRINCESS ELIZ COUSIN ELIZ YR WRK AT B. PK NVR

Studying it, Bud said, "Thanks, Howie, but can you make sense of that?"

"No, not really. Maybe the word *forgotten* and *princess* and *your work* at someplace or other, but it's Greek to me. But we need to get going. See you later, Sheriff."

"And no railroad cars in Price," Bud admonished Chance.

"Nope," Chance replied. "We're going to be too busy to do any graffing."

"Watch out for dire bears up on Ford Ridge," Bud said.

"We will, though I know you're just kidding, Sheriff. Right?"

Bud laughed as they walked out the door, Maureen coming to refill his coffee cup.

"You going to have lunch, Bud?" she asked.

"I should get back to work, but go ahead and bring me the special, please."

"Wilma Jean outdid herself this time," Maureen replied. "The enchiladas are nice and crisp."

As he waited for lunch, Bud again studied the note. He knew Morse code required that one use abbreviations in order to make the transmission as short as possible, since you were spelling out words, but Howie's translation made no sense.

But as he studied it closer and closer, something dawned on him: he'd assumed the message would go from the right hand to the left, but what if it was the other way around?

He cut the message in two and flipped the words to where it read:

-.-. --- ..- ... .. -. / . .-.. .. --.. / -.-- .-. / .-- .-. -.- / .- / -... .--.- / .-. -.- / -. ..- .-. /
..-. .-. --. - -. / .--. .-. .. -. -.-. . ... / . .-.. .. --..

COUSIN ELIZ YR WRK AT B. PK NVR FRGTN PRINCESS ELIZ

Bingo! It still didn't make perfect sense, but now it at least hinted at some kind of actual message: *Cousin Eliz your work at B. Pk never forgotten Princess Eliz*

Where was B. Pk and who was Princess Eliz?

He leaned back, distracted, as Maureen served the enchiladas. Hadn't Elizabeth, the one married to Cy, said she'd been named for her grandmother, who was named for Britain's Queen Elizabeth? Could this Princess Elizabeth have been the same Elizabeth who later became Queen?

It would make sense, since most princesses do end up queens.

And yes, the mittens would be quite a museum piece if knit by royalty, especially in Canada, which was still a commonwealth, a former British territory and still valued the historical connection. And it would also explain why Cy's Elizabeth wanted them back, for they would be a valuable piece of her family heritage. Maybe they were related to royalty, if her grandmother and Queen Elizabeth were cousins.

Savoring the hot enchiladas, Bud wondered why Cy would want the mittens, and once again, who the Grandfathers were. And what work was the knitter referring to? Had Elizabeth's grandmother contributed something important to Queen Elizabeth? If so, why would she be rewarded with a simple pair of mittens, ones with a secret embedded code?

It all seemed too complicated, Bud thought, finishing up his lunch. He needed some Big Empty time, time out wandering the big sweeping desert that bounded Green River.

Hadn't some Chinese philosopher once said that a wise man knows it's better to sit on the banks of a remote mountain stream than to be emperor of the whole world? He would get the dogs and, since Green River wasn't especially known for mountain streams, they would go look for pigeon-blood agate down some desert wash, all this Morse code and dire bear stuff forgotten.

19

Bud had brought his camera, and he recalled the rabbitbrush as being especially colorful when he'd gone up Tusher Canyon, so he decided to go there again and hopefully get some nice photos. Maybe he'd find something else of importance where he'd found Christian's radio, though he figured he'd probably rather not.

Driving up the canyon, its walls getting higher and higher, he began to feel that sense of freedom that always came with wandering in the desert, no destination in mind and nowhere to be.

But it wasn't long before his sense of well-being slipped away, for in the road ahead sat a brown pickup with a white topper and Saskatchewan plates.

He stopped, but no one was around, so he continued on until he finally saw a figure walking in the distance. He could tell from the slightly stooped shoulders that it was Cy.

He wasn't surprised to see that Cy had retrieved the pickup, but he was surprised to see him in Tusher Canyon, for he would've bet that the old guy was back up on the plateau, looking for the elusive Grandfathers, whatever they were.

He pulled up next to Cy and motioned for him to get into the FJ, scooting Lindie into the back with Hoppie and Pierre.

"Afternoon," Bud said. "Nice day for a walk, eh?"

"Every time I drive that dang truck, it breaks down," Cy replied, getting in.

"That may be why your wife doesn't want you to drive it," Bud replied, grinning.

"It breaks down with her, too," Cy said desultorily.

"You going anyplace in particular?" Bud asked.

"Not really," Cy replied. "Just out to see the world."

"Well, then you're here for the same reason I am," Bud said. "There's an old stock tank up here where I want to stop and let the dogs out for a while. They like to sniff around. It's our way of decompressing."

"Things pretty busy back there in town?" Cy asked.

"Not really," Bud replied. "It's just an excuse to get out. I was hoping for some juoksentelisinkohan time."

"I won't even ask," Cy replied.

With that, he pulled up to the canyon wall where some cattleman had channelled a small spring, old pipes running into a small metal tank where water striders skimmed around. Bud let the dogs out, who immediately began sniffing everything while he and Cy sat on nearby rocks.

Bud asked, "Do you mind if I ask what you're really doing out here? Are you looking for something?"

Cy looked irritated, and Bud had decided he wasn't going to answer when he finally replied.

"Sheriff, look at these water striders here. They live on the surface of the water, using the surface tension to walk around, and some are born with wings and some are born without. If the waters dry up, the ones with wings can just fly to another water source and carry on, but the ones without wings are out of luck."

Bud nodded his head as Cy continued.

"So, you'd think it would be better to have wings, right? But the ones without wings have a better daily life because they're not dealing with heavy wings, carrying them around and having to protect them. They can move around easier and get to food sources quicker, and they have more babies."

Now silent, Bud decided Cy must be finished, though not sure what his point was. Maybe he just liked entomology. As he turned his camera on to see if he could photograph a strider, Cy continued.

"So, which is better? Having a better daily life and maybe facing your food source drying up, or having harder daily lives and being able to move if you need to? I don't know the answer, but I do know that it's good we have both types, because striders are an important food source for other things, such as birds and fish, plus they love to eat mosquitoes."

Bud wasn't sure what to say.

"You don't see too many water striders out here in the desert," he finally replied. "Primarily because there isn't very much water."

Cy continued. "Sheriff, me and Elizabeth, we're like those water striders with the big heavy wings. And Christian and his generation and kids, they're like the ones that are carefree and footloose. The heavy wings we carry are called tradition. We're responsible for carrying it from our ancestors to our children. But what do you do if your children aren't so interested in the traditions? It's a heavy burden, one you can't just toss off lightly, because it's what grounds us. The kids, they just don't realize that yet. But knowing who we are gives us a foundation for a good life."

"You're lucky you still have the old traditions," Bud said.

"I know," Cy replied. "And I know you've been wondering why I want to run around in wild places where nobody goes. See, Sheriff, I'm a Cree elder. Part of my job is protecting the old traditions. I helped uncover a ribstone at the Wanuskewin, and I'm convinced there are Grandfathers here in the States. If so, it would prove we once came here in our wanderings. My people's wings took us to many places."

Bud said thoughtfully, "Cy, I won't ask what the Grandfathers are or what the Wanuskewin is because I know you won't tell me. But it's OK, I don't really need to know."

Cy replied, "Wanuskewin Heritage Park is no secret. Wanuskewin is from the nēhiyawēwin or Plains Cree and means *sanctuary,* or *seeking peace of mind,* and has been a sacred site and gathering place for the people of the Northern Plains for more than 6,000 years. It's near Saskatoon and not far from Swift Current. I was out there one day looking around and found a place where the resident buffalo herd, or bison, as you call them, had rolled around and uncovered a large rock. It was a ribstone."

Cy paused, watching the striders, then added, "A ribstone is a boulder with grooves carved into it that represent ribs, a petroglyph representing an animal's rib cage, and this one also had a small spirit figure carved onto it, all associated with the bison hunt. Archeologists later uncovered a larger stone there with a grid pattern, which they say is associated with a vision quest."

He added, "It's a style known as the hoofprint tradition, which was common in southern Alberta and Saskatchewan, as well as North and South Dakota, Montana, and Wyoming. Instead of carving an entire bison, they carved motifs such as hooves or ribs. We elders call such rocks *Grandfathers.* They're sacred. We normally don't talk about them."

"And you think you'll find them around here?" Bud asked. "Do you have a reason to think that? It sounds like we may be a bit too far south."

"They're here. I just need to keep looking. But some think these petroglyphs belong to the Pit and Groove Style, which dated to around 20,000 years ago and is the earliest example of indigenous people in North America. But the rock I found, it was very unusual. It had black paintings on its sides—one of a starburst and another of an animal figure with a long tail. This kind of stuff is unprecedented in Canadian rock art."

He paused, then added, "But Christian left his radio out here, and I need to find it. Can we go on up to the petroglyph panel?"

"Why would he leave it out here?" Bud asked.

"He had to go get better cell reception to take a work call."

"But why leave the radio?"

"He didn't want to compromise the fox."

"What about the mittens?" Bud asked.

"How do you know about the mittens?" Cy asked.

"Elizabeth said you took something important from a museum, Cy, something that technically belonged to her. Was it the mittens?"

Cy, looking disturbed, said, "Yes, it was the mittens. She loaned them to the museum. How do you know about them?"

"Why are they so important?" Bud asked, dodging Cy's question.

"The mittens have a secret code that shows that she and her family are related to the crown, but they also have a message just for me. Besides, I wanted Elizabeth around. All she wants to do is take care of the grandbabies, and I knew that if I took the mittens, she'd want to spend some time with me, even if just to harangue me."

"Was the bear that followed you and Christian a dream, Cy, or was it a person you'd rather not implicate?"

"Let's go look for that radio," Cy replied, standing. "And there was a bear, Sheriff. It was huge. It was a light brown, shone in the moonlight, and had something shiny around its neck."

"Like a radio collar?" Bud asked. "And I do believe you really did see a bear, Cy, I'm just not convinced it was when and where you said you did."

"Let's go look for that radio," Cy repeated.

"No need," Bud replied. "My friend Howie has it, and I have the mittens."

"You have them? That's great. I can get them back now."

"No, they're staying in my safe until I find out who they really belong to."

"They're Elizabeth's."

Bud replied, "Cy, I know there's more going on than you wanting the mittens. Maybe if you tell me, I can be of help. It seems like someone's out to get Christian, or maybe they want something you have. That wasn't a bear that slammed him. There were no bear tracks. And someone searched his truck. Does it have something to do with the fox hunters? And are you looking for something besides the Grandfathers?"

Cy replied quietly, "Let's go figure out what's wrong with Elizabeth's truck."

Bud gathered up the dogs, and they were soon headed back down the canyon, Cy's face holding a look of surprise mixed with frustration.

20

Bud sat in the customer waiting room at Green River Automotive, if one could call it a waiting room, for it mostly held stacks of tires for sale and a few old lawn chairs with some outdated magazines about raising goats and an equally outdated and empty coffee pot.

Cy sat across from him, munching on the last snickerdoodle cookie from the paper plate next to the coffee pot. Mrs. Jensen had spied Bud's FJ and delivered the cookies to the shop, which at first made Bud happy, but after seeing them quickly disappear into the hands of Cy and Art, the shop owner, he'd kind of wished she'd waited until he'd been back at his office. He didn't mind sharing if it meant he also got a few, but he'd only managed to get two out of the dozen or so.

The truck had needed a new alternator, which Art happily had in stock and could install while they waited, which to Bud was a good thing, though Cy was worried it would cost an arm and a leg. Bud knew that Art was fair and honest, so he'd encouraged Cy to get the job done, and what choice did the old guy have, anyway, since he needed a vehicle?

At this point, Bud was hoping Cy would decide to go on up to

Christian's in Salt Lake and give up whatever mission he seemed to be on, especially since the rest of his family had flown the coop.

There was nothing cheap enough in Green River for Cy in terms of lodging, who Bud knew had little to no money, unless Bud were to offer the use of their Airstream out in the back yard. He knew his wife would frown on the offer, since there was really no reason for him to stay.

As Cy finished off the last snickerdoodle, Art emerged from the back of the shop, asking, "You play a lot of hockey?"

Cy, looking puzzled, replied, "You think I play hockey because I have Canada plates?"

Art laughed. "No, because the back of your rig has a bunch of hockey sticks in it. Anyway, it's all done."

Cy replied, "My wife always carries extra hockey sticks in case any of the kids find themselves in a game. The kids where we live play a lot of street hockey in the winter, nothing else for them to do. Besides, a stick comes in handy for reaching things in the back of your truck."

"Great idea," Art replied. "Maybe I should get one."

"Help yourself," Cy offered. "There's plenty there."

"I counted twenty," Art replied. "I've never seen one hockey stick in person, and you have twenty. I really would like one, if you're serious."

"Twenty?" Cy replied. "I wondered what was rattling around back there. So how much do I owe you?"

"Can I take a few?" Art asked. "That way, if it ever really freezes in Green River, we can start a team."

"Sure," Cy replied. "Take all of them—well, leave a couple so I can reach stuff in the truck. Sticks are a dime a dozen in Canada. I can get more."

"I'm going to sell you the alternator at cost and throw in the install for free," Art replied. "In exchange for the sticks. Man, think of it! A hockey team in Green River. How many are on a team?"

"Six, including a goalie," Cy replied. "Three forwards and two defensemen. You'll have enough sticks for three teams. That's eighteen, so leave me two."

"We could flood the town park once it starts to freeze," Bud offered. "Since there aren't any ponds or lakes or anything around here."

"Snowball could be the mascot," Art said.

"Who's that?" Cy asked.

"One of my goats. She's pure white. What should we call the team?"

"How about the Green River Pirates?" Cy said.

"That's already the name of the high school sports team," Art replied. "How about the Green River Lizards?"

"Fits the area, but a hockey team?" Bud laughed.

"Green River Misfits," Art said. "Because a hockey team in the desert is definitely a misfit kind of thing."

"Who will they play?" Bud asked. "You're going to need to get this hockey thing to spread across the country if you want to have real games."

"I think it's already spread, Bud," Art said.

"Probably be a short season," Cy said. "Does it ever snow here?"

"Not much snow, but it can get cold," Art replied. "Where can we get pucks? How about the Green River Penguins?"

"I think there's already a team named that," Bud said. "In Pittsburgh."

"They call themselves the Green River Penguins?" Cy asked.

"You can be the ref," Art said. "You'll go a long way with that sense of humor."

Bud stood, saying, "I'm going to leave you guys to your devices. I need to get back to work. Cy, your wife's probably wondering where you are, so maybe get in touch with her. Better still, go on up to Christian's. I don't want to worry about you getting lost."

"I won't get lost," Cy replied, standing. "As soon as I pay Art here, I'm getting a motel in Price. Christian's coming down tomorrow. But I'm going to stop by your office first, Sheriff. You have something that belongs to my family."

"If you're thinking it's what I'm thinking, it's off limits until I do some research, like I told you," Bud replied.

"What in hell's bells are you two talking about?" Art asked.

"Your sheriff confiscated something that belongs to me," Cy replied, handing Art his credit card. "See if I have anything left on this."

Art, running the card, said, "Thanks for the hockey sticks. If you're ever down this way, stop in and we'll make you the honorary something or other for whatever game we're playing."

"Sounds good," Cy replied, walking out the door with Bud. "Until then, keep your stick on the ice."

As they went outside, Cy said, "Sheriff, I'm going to meet you at your office. I want to see the mittens, just to make sure they're the right ones, and that's all I ask. Just show them to me, and I'll leave in peace."

Bud replied, "How many pairs of mittens do you think are lying around some desert canyon when it's not even winter?"

"They're purple, right? With lightning bolts?"

"That sounds right."

"I'll meet you at your office," Cy insisted. "I could use a good cup of coffee before I head up the road. You do have coffee, don't you?"

Bud sighed. "Alright, Cy. Come on by and I'll show you the mittens and make you some coffee, but you're not taking them with you."

"I have no such intention, Sheriff," Cy replied, scooting into the cab of Elizabeth's pickup. "See you there."

21

Bud had put the coffeepot on, and as it gurgled, he unlocked the safe and took the mittens out. He'd take a closer look before Cy showed up, which should be any minute.

Just then, his phone rang.

"Yell-ow, Bud speaking."

"Bud, it's Maureen. Have you seen Howie?"

"Not since earlier. Is everything OK?"

"I'm really worried. He was supposed to be back way before this. He needs to get over to the drive-in. He said he and some guy were going up to Price to look at a retriever. We've talked about getting a dog, and I thought we decided it was too soon, that we should wait until Mal's a little older, but that's what he said he was doing."

Bud laughed. "He's looking at a repeater, Maureen, not a retriever."

"What's a repeater?"

"It's one of those towers you see up on the mountaintops—has to do with ham radio. He met some guy in Price who helps maintain the club's repeater and invited him up. I'm sure he's fine, just running late."

Maureen sighed. "That's a relief. Tell him to call if you see him."

"Will do."

His mind back on the mittens, Bud placed them on his desk. It seemed odd that a pair of mittens possibly knit by a British princess would be here in Green River, but he'd heard of stranger things, like the time he'd found a diamond from Australia.

He again marveled at how soft and well-knit they were. He should make sure they were well-protected by keeping them in an evidence bag, he decided, pulling one from his desk drawer.

Picking the mittens up, he noticed one of the thumbs felt stiff and different from the other. As he turned it inside-out to investigate, a piece of folded paper fell out. Unfolding it, he read what looked like a set of coordinates:

39.1600493 -110.7159824

He wasn't sure what he was looking at, and he'd have to open up his computer and check it out. He stuck the piece of paper in his pocket just as Cy walked in the door.

As Bud offered him a cup of coffee, the old guy sat down and began examining the mittens. Bud watched closely, and sure enough, Cy began feeling each thumb as if looking for the piece of paper. Finally, finding nothing, he leaned back and sipped his coffee, looking disappointed and tired.

"I think you need to get on back to Price and get a motel room," Bud said. "I'd offer you the house, but my wife is having some painting done."

"I'm OK," Cy replied. "That was really nice of you to let me stay there, and to even stock the fridge. Sheriff, you seem like a really good guy."

Bud replied, "Thanks, Cy, I appreciate that, but I'm still not giving you the mittens."

"They belong to my wife," Cy replied. "But was there anything else with them?"

Ignoring the question, Bud asked, "Can you tell me more about this supposed bear that attacked Christian? What exactly did you see?"

"It was dark, so not much. Didn't really see it except later, over in the trees at the edge of the meadow, but it was huge."

"But you said it was following you guys after you got stuck and left the car."

"Something was following us."

"Would it have anything to do with fox hunting?"

Cy was silent, then said, "Probably not."

Bud asked, "Are you pretty familiar with bears? Do you have many in Saskatchewan?"

"Enough that I know what one looks like. We do have grizzlies, though the last one was supposed to have been shot in 1956. It's not very well known, but they have been spotted in the Wild Cat Hills, which is a wilderness area in the northeast. But we have plenty of black bears. We even supposedly have a few Grolar Bears."

"What's that?" Bud asked.

"It's a grizzly and polar bear hybrid. The two look very different but are so closely related that hybridization can occur. Polar bears aren't native to Saskatchewan and have only been sighted near the Manitoba border, where barrenground grizzlies and polar bears overlap. Barrenground grizzlies are a different subspecies from the plains grizzlies which roamed the prairies following the bison."

Bud replied, "Are you especially interested in bears or something? You seem to know a lot about them."

"My grandson's a biologist. He knows a lot about bears. We've had some good talks. I find it interesting."

"Christian?"

"Yes. He works for the Forest Service. He has a degree from Montana State University. His mom's from the States, so he's a dual citizen. Our son is Christian's dad, and they live in Bozeman. Christian and his family moved to Salt Lake when he got the state job."

Bud thought of the conversation Elizabeth had overheard between Maddie and Auggie about the bear.

"Is Christian studying bears on the plateau by any chance?"

Cy was quiet for awhile, then answered, "Not really. He wanted to go up there because he'd heard reports of a strange bear being seen, but he wasn't on any kind of assignment or anything like that. He was actually on vacation, going to the fancy dance in Delta, though we were a bit off-track."

"I thought it was your idea to go up there to look for the Grandfathers."

"I don't remember saying that was our reason, though I was all for looking there. You can't try to find the Grandfathers, as they will elude you until they want to be found."

"Well, hang on here a minute, and I'll see if I can help you out," Bud said, opening his laptop. He was soon keying in the coordinates from the piece of paper.

"I don't know what the deal is with this place, but it's the MK Tunnels, over on the San Rafael Swell. The Department of Defense dug some tunnels there to detonate and study explosives after World War II. They've been gated for the most part, or caved in, and their name comes from Morrison Knudsen, the contractors."

He handed Cy the paper he'd taken from the mittens. "I suspect this is what you're looking for?"

"Some tunnels?" Cy asked, perplexed, taking the small piece of paper and looking at the coordinates. "Christian wanted me to find this for some reason."

"I doubt if this has anything to do with bears," Bud said. "What exactly are you guys looking for, anyway? Something that's going to get you into trouble?"

"It already has," Cy replied, sticking the paper into his shirt pocket. "It already has."

With that, he walked out the door, just as Howie and Chance entered.

22

"Have you ever heard a hotdog play the *Banana Boat Song*, Bud?" Howie asked, sitting down and putting his feet on a nearby chair.

"I'm not even sure what that is, Howie," Bud replied, motioning toward another nearby chair. "Have a seat, Chance."

"It's that old song about some poor guy loading bananas down wherever they grow bananas. It goes, *Day-oh, Day-oh, Daylight come and me wan' go home.* You know, the one by Harry Belafonte."

Bud nodded, "Sure, that song from Jamaica. That goes way back, but wouldn't it be more appropriate to have a banana play it instead of a hot dog?"

Howie replied, "I don't know. A fruit might not work."

"So, you overcook a hotdog until it's hard, and then you carve out the interior and cut holes in it? Kind of like a flute?" Bud asked. "Does it have to be kosher?"

Howie laughed. "No, it's a totally unmodified hotdog—well, it is until you're done playing the *Banana Boat Song* on it anyway. Then it kind of turns into a piece of carbon."

"It's pure science," Chance said. "It was amazing."

Howie added, "We had a great time with Jim, the guy from the museum. We drove up on Ford Ridge there above Price and helped him do some work on their club repeater."

"You haven't seen a view until you've been up there," Chance said.

"Well," Howie continued. "There's a bunch of radio towers up there, and one of them belongs to the local AM station. It has a big fence around it with all kinds of *Danger Keep Out High Voltage* signs, and for good reason. It'll fry your beans if you get too close. So Jim decided to show us why we shouldn't get too close. We'd been having a picnic, and we had some leftover hotdogs, so he wrapped some wire around the end of a really long tree limb, then grounded it using his jumper cables, put a hotdog on the wire, then stuck it through the fence and touched the tower with it."

"Sounds dangerous," Bud said.

"It gives new meaning to ham radio," Chance said reverently.

Howie continued. "The hot dog started transmitting the *Banana Boat Song*. I mean, you could make out the words and everything. It was really loud, kind of like a radio turned up high. It then started talking about some tire shop in Price, then arced and burned the end off."

"If you use two hotdogs, you'd have stereo," Chance added. "But I've often wondered why sometimes the radio signal goes in and out, especially during your favorite song, and now I know. It's someone cooking hotdogs!"

"This really happened?" Bud asked skeptically. "How does that work?"

Howie said patiently, "Any metal can resonate at the right frequency and demodulate a radio frequency."

"I'm not sure what that means," Bud replied.

"It's simple, Sheriff," Howie replied. "The original radio signal is encoded within a carrier wave at a specific frequency. When you get a conductive object, something that the radio wave can move through, this radio signal, which is the music or whatever from the station, comes through the object at harmonics or multiples of the original carrier frequency and you can hear the audio. It's due to electromagnetic induction."

"Did that make sense to you, Chance?" Bud asked.

"Not really," Chance replied. "But it was something to behold. A hotdog playing music! Talking to your food is one thing, but when it talks back, you ask it, 'What the fridge are you up to?'"

"I need to put that on my cuss-words list," Howie said. "But people with loose fillings have been known to hear radio stations. When two different metal fillings are at the right distance apart, they can act like a crude tuned capacitor and the jawbone carries the sound directly to the ear. And people who live near powerful radio station towers will hear the radio on their bedsprings and washing machines and the speakers on their clock radios, and sometimes even on light bulbs and wire fences."

He added, "You know the station KOA, called the 50,000 Watt Blowtorch of the Rockies? It's been in Denver since the 1920s. You go into the building there and you can hear the station broadcasting without even needing a speaker. Metal objects in the building pick up the signal, acting like antennas."

"Sounds like you guys had a good time," Bud replied.

"Tell him what else you did," Chance said to Howie.

Howie paused, then said, "Sheriff, I'm not sure if this is going to go over well with Maureen or not, but I made a little purchase when we were up in Price."

"She called, by the way," Bud said. "She's worried about you and wants you to call her."

"I should do that," Howie said sheepishly. "This is why we're so late, Sheriff—I bought a caboose. This guy at the museum, Jim, he said he had one sitting on his farm that was there when he bought the place. He sold it to me real cheap. I'm going to have to get a flatbed truck and some kind of hoist to get it on the truck, but then I'm bringing it here."

"That's really something," Bud said approvingly. "What kind of shape is it in?"

"It's in really good shape, or will be after me and Chance paint it all up. I'm going to set it out behind the house and make it into my radio shack. Chance is going to do some train graffiti on it for me, and I'll put my call sign over the front door."

"I think that's fantastic, Howie," Bud said.

"And something else, Bud, I'm going to legally change my name to my call sign, WØRQC."

"Why would you do that?" Bud asked.

"Well, it's like this," Howie replied. "When I'm operating the radio a bunch, you know, you have to say your call sign a lot, and when I go through the drive-through somewhere or into a coffee shop and they ask me my name, I forget and give my call sign. They look at me all weird, and then I realize that I gave my call sign instead of saying 'Howie,' then I have to explain. It usually gets awkward because nobody gets it. If I change my name to my call sign, I won't screw up, plus I don't have to worry about somebody else with the same name picking up my coffee."

"You've had that happen before?" Chance asked.

"Well, only when I use the name Spartacus," Howie replied.

"I don't get it," Chance said.

"Never mind," Howie replied. "It's from this movie where they're trying to find this guy named Spartacus and everyone around him says they're Spartacus so they can't figure out who the real Spartacus is—forget it, it was a dumb joke. But Bud, there's something else that happened when we were up there, I mean *way* up there on Ford Ridge. You can see the whole plateau from up there, and there's even an old bristlecone pine forest, but we were just standing there when we heard the weirdest sound ever."

Chance said excitedly, "It was really strange. Give you nightmares."

Howie continued. "It was coming from far away, so it had to be big for the sound to carry like that. Sheriff, it was a loud roar, like you'd hear in some Grizzly Adams movie just before he gets eaten."

"Did he get eaten?" Chance asked.

"I don't know, but Jim said there's been reports of some kind of really big bear roaming around the plateau. A couple of Jim's friends said they saw it up close and it was terrifying. They're never going up there again, according to Jim."

Bud leaned back in his chair, thinking of how Shorty had felt they were being watched, as well as the sheepherder who'd been injured by a bear. Maybe it was time to call Sheriff Davis and find out more.

"That's concerning, Howie," Bud said. "Probably a good idea to stay off the plateau."

"Done," Howie replied. "But I need to call my wife, so we need to head on out. Chance is going to start doing a mural on the drive-in tomorrow. I'm letting him camp in our barn. He's going to be busy, with that and the caboose and some windows for Melon Days."

As they walked out the door, Chance turned to Bud and said, "I forgot to tell you I got to say hello to the moon. But seriously, that bear or whatever it was, it was *huge*. I'm glad I'm not up there. Sleeping in a barn sounds pretty good—and safe."

"Except for Howie's two cats, watch out for them. But you fellas have a good night," Bud said, battening down the hatches so he could go on home for the day, and like Chance, glad he wasn't camping on the plateau.

23

It was later that evening, and Bud leaned back in his leather recliner in the bungalow's living room, Wilma Jean half asleep on the nearby plaid couch she'd bought at the thrift store up in Price, Pierre and Hoppie curled up at her side.

Lindie lay on a rug at Bud's feet, and he made a note to himself to be careful to not catch her up in the footrest when he closed the recliner, thinking of how Frosty got caught in his couch.

"That was really sweet of you to fix dinner tonight, hon," Wilma Jean said, looking over the top of her paperback book, *West with the Night*, about the legendary pilot Beryl Markham.

"It was nothing," Bud replied. "I should do it more often and give you a break. I can fix whatever you bring home from the Melon Rind any time you want. It always turns out great."

Wilma Jean laughed. "Those enchiladas warmed up nicely, didn't they?"

"There's even some left for lunch tomorrow," Bud said. "But answer me this. Why would anyone leave a note with a set of coordinates in the thumb of a mitten?"

"I don't even want to know what latest thing you're working on," she replied. "It sounds too complicated, and it's late. But maybe they were trying to hide the note from someone who they knew would never put on the mittens. It would actually be a pretty good hiding place."

"But why coordinates?"

"What do they go to?"

"The MK Tunnels."

"You mean over on the Swell? I thought those were all gated now, or blasted shut."

"I thought so, too," Bud replied. "These mittens had the coordinates and nothing else. No explanation, nothing—well, except for a message written in Morse code."

"Where did you find them? Do you know who they belong to? Morse code?"

"They were out in Tusher Canyon, and yes, they belong to the grandmother of the guy who hid them."

"Well, why not ask him?"

"I probably should," Bud conceded. "Except he's not around to ask. But I think it has something to do with a bear roaming around on the Wasatch Plateau. Reports are saying it's huge, and Sheriff Davis up in Price said it's injured someone. I think me and Shorty may have been in its vicinity when we were up there."

Wilma Jean sat up straight, the book falling onto her lap. "Bud, you be careful. I thought you were done over there, now that we've found the missing guy, Christian, and his grandfather. Is he the one who you're referring to?"

"The one who knows what the coordinates are for? Yes, Christian. His grandfather, Cy, won't tell me anything, but I suspect he also knows."

Wilma Jean asked, "Why would they be interested in the MK Tunnels? That's not even close to the plateau. The tunnels are over by Buckhorn Wash. I can't really picture a bear wanting to hang out there, as it's mostly just Navajo sandstone and desert. No trees or anything much."

"It's definitely not bear country," Bud said. "But this bear doesn't sound like anything we've seen before around here. It's supposed to be huge—and aggressive. This sounds like a grizzly, or even something else."

"What do you mean, something else?"

"Like a big polar bear-grizzly mix—that's a real thing, you know."

"Good Lord! On the plateau? And killing people?"

Bud replied, "I know, though it hasn't killed anyone yet. It's pretty concerning. But why the MK Tunnels?"

"Look, hon, the tunnels are gated off as far as I know. How many are there, anyway?" Wilma Jean asked.

"I'm not sure," Bud replied. "But I think Morrison Knudson blasted out three. One was 1,000 feet long, and they conducted blasts that blew its top in. The other two are smaller and maybe more intact."

"Maybe someone's doing experiments and using one of the tunnels as a base," Wilma Jean said. "Just how far is it from there over to the plateau?"

Bud thought for a moment, then replied, "As the crow flies, it's only about 15 miles from the tunnels to Castle Dale, so it's not really all that far. And you may not know this, but Christian's a biologist with the state. But there's more. Someone's following them, and I suspect whoever it is, they want those coordinates."

"But why?"

"I don't know, but I think they're the ones who slammed Christian and bruised his ribs."

"He said it was a bear," Wilma Jean said, now sitting up and stroking Pierre's soft dachshund ears, the little dog looking like he was in Heaven, while Hoppie tried to get in on the action, pushing his nose into her hand.

"I think it may be someone they're trying to protect," Bud said.

"Protect someone who would mess up Christian's ribs?"

"I don't understand it," Bud said. "But there were all these fox hunters out there, and maybe they had something to do with it."

"Yes," Wilma Jean said. "Molly came into the cafe and was telling me all about them. But Bud, it wouldn't be all that hard for me to fly over the tunnels and scout them out, if you want. You could come with me."

"Thanks for the offer, but I'd just get in the way," Bud replied, now pushing the recliner upright, disturbed by the thought of flying and thereby forgetting about Lindie, who, caught in the footrest, began yelping. Bud quickly opened it, petting her and saying he was sorry while she gave him a dirty look and went to Wilma Jean.

"Maybe you could have Howie or Shorty fly over there with you," Bud suggested, trying to get Lindie to come to him.

Wilma Jean stood. "Maybe someday you'll get over this flying thing, spread your wings, and take to the sky."

"That's from that song *Summertime*, isn't it?" Bud asked. "I'm like that little baby in the song—thinking of flying makes me want to cry."

Wilma Jean laughed and took his hand, pulling him up. "Put the dogs out for a minute, then let's go to bed. I'll fly over the tunnels tomorrow while you play stick with the dogs out at the farm."

"I'm kind of lying low," Bud replied, opening the patio door to the back yard and letting the dogs out. "Until the harvest is over."

"That's fine," Wilma Jean replied. "But hon, promise me you'll stay away from the Wasatch Plateau."

"I can't picture any reason to go up there," Bud said, glad he was far from the plateau and its mysteries.

He let the dogs back in, and they all went to bed.

24

Bud sat in his office, feeling like he was finally getting recentered after all the uncertainty of dealing with Cy and things on the plateau. He hoped that Wilma Jean flying over the MK Tunnels would maybe give him something to work with regarding the note with the coordinates.

She'd gotten up early and was probably already on her way back, as she and Maureen were catering an anniversary party that evening.

He thought again of the sheepherder who'd been mauled on the plateau. He'd never been much of a fan of bears, and knowing a dangerous bear was out there had made him worry more than he'd realized. He was glad the sheepherder's mauling had happened in Carbon County instead of in his jurisdiction, though he actually wished it hadn't happened anywhere.

He knew that dealing with the bear itself was the job of the wildlife people, and now he could get back to doing what he did best, ensuring that the people of Green River and Emery County had their well-deserved peace and quiet. His constituency expected very little from him, and it was his job to deliver it.

He pulled his harmonica from his pocket, thinking it was time for a new song, as *Red River Valley*, *Ghost Riders in the Sky*, and the other cowboy songs from his youth were getting old, plus he couldn't really seem to master them like he wanted.

He'd totally given up on the yodeling one, and now he decided to try *Summertime*, as he knew that would make Wilma Jean happy, as it was one of her favorites.

He fiddled with the harmonica, humming the tune—*spread your wings, and take to the sky*—as he watched the action at Howie's Drive-In across the street, where a little red Radio Flyer wagon sat, filled with various colors of spray cans.

Chance was busy painting a mural on the drive-in wall next to the parking lot, stopping every so often to look at the wagon and ponder on which color he wanted to use next. Bud wasn't sure what he was making, but it was starting to kind of look like a radio tower with zigzag radio waves emanating out.

Every once in awhile, someone would stop to offer their advice or ask what he was doing, and Bud could tell he enjoyed sharing his art. Maybe someday he could be an art teacher or something, Bud mused, which would definitely pay better than doing railroad graffiti, though maybe not by much.

His phone rang.

"Yell-ow," he answered. "Sheriff's office."

"Bud?" A voice asked tentatively.

"It is," Bud replied. "Can I help you?"

"Bud, it's Sheriff Davis, up in Price."

"Good morning. I was thinking about calling you."

"I've been out on vacation, but now that I'm back I've been meaning to call and find out how things went with your search and rescue up on the plateau."

Bud replied, "I talked to Deputy Sam Wiggins and asked him to pass on that we found the people. Both parties ended up in the hospital, but nothing serious."

Davis paused, then said, "Well, you know how Sam is, but that's good news."

"I'm curious about that sheepherder that got mauled up your way," Bud said.

"Well, it's pretty simple. The guy was up on Clear Creek and apparently a bear came out of the forest, the horse reared up and threw him, and he was mauled, but not too badly. Apparently something distracted the bear, though he wasn't sure what. He said it sounded like some kind of music."

"Music? That's odd," Bud said, watching Chance now paint what looked like a flying saucer coming off one of the rays from the tower, a cadre of kids having gathered, watching with great interest as Bud realized it was supposed to be a giant hamburger.

"Yeah, he said the music was coming from the bear. I would normally be thinking he was drinking a little too much tequila, though I know the guy, and he's a good worker. He's from Peru—Feliciano Sanchez. Anyway, he described the bear, and it sounds like a pretty big black bear to me. But the Forest Service is investigating it because apparently Jack Peroulis, who has the sheep lease up there, was supposed to get his herd off two weeks ago and failed to do so. Feliciano wasn't even supposed to be up there. Peroulis is headed for a big fine, which wouldn't be his first. They've had trouble with him for years, and I think this may be the last time. He's going to lose his allotments."

"Why did they want the sheep off?" Bud asked. "Usually the leases go to the end of September, don't they?"

"Yeah, but this year they're pulling them off early because of the drought. Peroulis is pretty well-known for trying to milk every little bit out of everything. He doesn't take care of his herders, which he's legally required to do. He has a number of allotments, including one at Joe's Valley. Last year, his herders said he confiscated their visas and passports, rationed their food, and refused them medical treatment. We had to go up on the plateau this spring because he was shooting in the direction of some hikers, trying to scare them into leaving. He's bad news, and I wish he'd go back to wherever he's from."

"I've heard the price of wool has dropped significantly," Bud said.

"Yes," Davis replied. "Synthetic fibers are cheaper. And people aren't eating much mutton. These sheepmen are hurting financially.

Some are getting desperate, as they're worried about having to sell out."

"How did they know he was doing all this? Most of those herders don't speak a word of English and could never complain."

"There's a fellow from over in Loma, Colorado who comes and visits the herders every so often. He used to be a sheepherder himself. He's from Chili and eventually became a citizen. He's retired and spends his time being an advocate. He brings them food from donors and checks on everybody. At one point, several of the sheepmen were cited by the Feds for violating the Department of Labor's rules, and one of them was even disallowed from bringing H-2A workers in to tend his sheep. They pay them almost nothing, so that's a big blow to a sheep business."

"Dave, one quick question. How big is this Peroulis guy? I found some tracks, but whoever made them wasn't real heavy."

"He's probably about six feet, weighs 180 or so."

"Does he wear hiking boots?"

Sheriff Davis laughed. "I have yet to see a sheepman, or any kind of rancher for that matter, in anything but cowboy boots, even in church, they just shine them up. But anyway, Bud, my wife and I are thinking about bringing the kids down for Melon Days, so maybe I'll see you then."

"Don't forget the parade Saturday morning."

"Sounds like fun."

Sheriff Davis was gone, just as Chance put the finishing touches on a giant ice-cream cone emanating from another ray coming from the radio tower, his crowd of approving kids watching with admiration as he started to paint what looked to be a giant taco emanating from another ray.

Bud again picked up his harmonica, just in time for his phone to again ring. It was Wilma Jean.

"Hon, I flew over the MK Tunnels. I took Howie's mother-in-law, Maureen's mom, with me. She's visiting and has never been in a small plane. She was thrilled. She loves coming up from Hanksville to take care of little Malcolm, and she says she can teach me how to make really fluffy cream puffs for the cafe, even make them look like swans."

"That's great," Bud replied, trying not to sound impatient. "But what did you see?"

"Nothing worth reporting back about. Just a couple of tourists kicking around taking photos, nothing else."

"Nothing? No signs of nefarious activity?"

Wilma Jean laughed. "Nope, unless you call Cold War detritus nefarious. Maybe it was, back in its day."

"Thanks for going out. What's today's special? Tacos?"

"Bud, you know I never have a taco special. It's beef stew with homemade rolls. But Maureen and I won't be at the cafe, as we're catering the Green's 50th anniversary party."

"Old Man Green? Is he married?"

"No," Wilma Jean laughed. "It's a different set of Greens. Buck and Marietta."

"I can stop by the cafe and get some stew, though, right?" Bud asked, watching as Chance finished painting the taco. He was somewhat amazed at how quickly the guy could paint things, but then, he remembered he'd been working on the railroad, where things don't stay put for long.

Chance had now started another tower ray, this one with what looked like a hotdog on its end. It wasn't long until he painted musical notes coming from it.

"Art imitates life," Bud said. "Or something like that."

"What?" Wilma Jean asked. "Stop by the cafe after five. I need to go. I'll probably be pretty late."

He hung up just as Shorty walked in the door.

Bud asked, "Do you think someone would mistake Christian's pickup for a federal rig with that antenna on top?"

"Why?" Shorty asked.

"Sheriff Davis said there's a disgruntled sheep rancher who runs his herds on the plateau and has been in trouble with the government. I'm wondering if he's the one who vandalized Christian's truck, thinking it was a Forest Service vehicle."

"And maybe searched to see if they were collecting info on him?" Shorty asked.

"Could be."

"But what about Cy saying they saw a bear?"

Bud replied, "Maybe both things happened. But have a seat. I need you to educate me on some geology-related stuff, if you have time."

"I have lots of time," Shorty laughed. "All the way back to the Big Bang."

"We probably don't need to go that far back," Bud replied. "Maybe just 20,000 years would be good."

25

"Bud, you're not talking geology, per se, but more like biology, though I guess paleontology fits in there somewhere, too."

Shorty looked thoughtful, as Bud said, "Well, we've all heard of Occam's razor. The simplest solution is usually the right one. But why is that?"

Shorty replied, "I don't know. Maybe because the universe is inherently lazy and doesn't want to make things more complicated than they have to be. But what makes you think of Occam's razor?"

Bud replied, "Well, everybody keeps talking about a huge bear up on the plateau, and we all know that there's only regular-sized black bears up there. But according to Occam's razor, the solution would be that there really is a big bear up there. What I want to know is why, and how did it get there? Do you think it grew up there?"

"I don't know. It seems kind of odd that you'd have a giant bear emerge from a population of regular black bears."

Bud asked, "Do you think someone introduced it? Especially since it has a radio collar?"

"How do you know it has a radio collar?"

"Cy talked about it wearing a necklace, and I just talked to Sheriff Davis up in Price, and he said that the sheepherder that was attacked was saved by music that distracted the bear. What was odd is that the music was supposedly coming from the bear."

Shorty snorted. "I hope it wasn't like that hot dog Howie talked about. It could be hard on the bear to be a radio receiver."

"Well," Bud replied. "I have a theory that maybe that radio collar made some kind of noise that distracted the bear, and the sheepherder interpreted it as music."

"Could be the radio collar was acting like a receiver."

Bud replied, "Radio collars have a transmitter, which sends out a unique frequency, but I don't know about receiving. But if there really is a giant bear and it does have a radio collar, and we could figure out what frequency it's on, Howie could track it."

Shorty said, "That's a lot of ifs. And he has to be in the vicinity of the bear, doesn't he? Why not just hang a medium-rare steak around your neck—you could have it come to you."

"How about that KrakenSDR, would that work?" Bud asked.

"I don't know, but maybe if the collar's transmitting a signal, the Kraken would pick it up. That would be much more effective than Howie's little radio because the Kraken can pick up signals a lot farther, especially with its numerous antennas. But what exactly are you going to do if you find out it is a big bear? Are you going back over there looking for it?"

Bud sighed. "Unless someone in my jurisdiction is mauled or injured by it, then I have no interest in tracking anything down. Even at that, it's actually in the province of the wildlife department. They're the ones that take care of things like that, not the sheriff. But that takes me back to wondering why there might be a giant bear roaming around the plateau."

He continued. "Shorty, the two paleontologists, Maddie and Auggie, mentioned sequencing dire bear DNA. You said earlier this is impossible with dinosaurs because of the time factor, but dire bears weren't that long ago."

Shorty replied, "DNA and RNA don't last very long, Bud. They have a half-life of about 550 years, which means half is disintegrated at that point, and in 1000 years all of it is gone. But there are cases where things are preserved when you wouldn't expect it. It does happen, like the insects in the Burgess Shale. Most fossils were preserved only because something catastrophic happened to immediately cover them. Otherwise things just slowly decay."

He continued. "Scientists have found potential DNA fragments in fossils, but no complete dinosaur DNA has been found that I know of. Even if DNA were found, the technology to piece together a complete genome and then develop a viable organism doesn't currently exist."

"But could we maybe re-create a dire bear?"

"I don't know, but I do know that there's been a lot of studies trying to bring back wooly mammoths. Researchers have found well-preserved woolly mammoth remains, including skin, in Siberian permafrost, where the DNA has been preserved because of the freezing and dehydration. They've reconstructed the woolly mammoth's genome. But it's not just a matter of obtaining the DNA, you also have to coax it to grow inside a cell. Bud, anything that went extinct more than a thousand years ago is most likely gone forever. That's the definition of extinct."

Shorty continued. "The real missing element here, the thing that nobody really knows how it works, is the environment that they lived in. We know that their world was quite different from ours today. Could Pleistocene animals survive in today's environment?"

Bud replied, "I read where it said there are a number of Pleistocene animals that didn't go extinct, like gray wolves and muskoxen. So if they can survive in today's environment, why not a dire bear?"

"Maybe one could, but we don't know how much these surviving species have had to adapt in the last 20,000 years. Could you bring back a mammoth from say 20,000 years ago and stick it up on the plateau and have it survive? Adaptation is an ongoing process, and as environments changed, the animals either adapted to them or died. So it's very possible that even if you brought back the dire bear it wouldn't be able to survive in the current environment on the plateau, even though it survived quite well 20,000 years ago. We aren't sure how much the environment has changed, though we do have a lot of clues. For example, a lot of the redrock country once was covered with ponderosa pine trees and looked quite different. We know this from packrat middens filled with seeds. As climate changes, the flora and fauna change with it, and the ones that don't adapt die out."

He continued. "Take the case of dire wolves. They became extinct about 13,000 years ago, and they were distinct enough from other canid species that they weren't able to interbreed, unlike coyotes and gray wolves. They didn't adapt to changes in the environment, and mixing with other species is one way to do this. The American lion and the dire bear had similar evolutionary patterns in North America, and they both went extinct at the same time. Some say they were hunted to extinction by humans, but scientists are starting to think it was more of an adaptation problem."

Bud replied, "Going by the conversation Elizabeth overheard between Auggie and Maddie, it sounds like they were trying to introduce something into the environment that got away from them. There are lots of cases where animals or plants brought into non-native environments wreaked havoc on everything. Maybe Maddie and Auggie were part of some kind of experiment to bring in a big bear and let it loose and see how it fared, like maybe a Grolar Bear."

Shorty said, "The biggest bears on Earth are the Kodiak and polar bears. A full-grown Kodiak bear can weigh over 2000 pounds and stand ten feet tall. Do you suppose they brought one in and put a radio collar on it so they could track it and see how it adapted? If so, they're playing with fire."

"I can't picture the wildlife department signing off on something like that," Bud said.

"Maybe they didn't. Christian works for the Forest Service, so maybe he'd heard rumors and was here to see what he could find. But it could just be a black bear that somehow mutated and outgrew its genes. I guess it's a good thing the Forest Service told the sheep ranchers to get their herds off the plateau early. A bear like that could decimate a whole herd in no time flat."

Bud asked, "What do Kodiak bears eat? Maybe that's part of the study to see if this bear that's used to a different ecosystem can adapt to this one. I mean, it would make sense to use the plateau as a testing ground because it sees so few people, though hunting season is starting. There may be a few bowhunters on the plateau that are in for a surprise."

He paused, then added, "I wonder what Maddie meant when she told Auggie she'd saved the sheepherder. That was part of the conversation Elizabeth overheard."

"I don't know," Shorty replied. "But I'm hoping neither of us has to go back up there. But Bud, I just remembered something that may be important, maybe not. A Kodiak bear has what's called a 'natal ring' around their neck for the first few years of life. It's white and really stands out. Maybe that's the necklace Cy talked about, not a radio collar."

"Interesting," Bud replied. "Something to think about, or maybe it had two collars. But Shorty, one last thing, a change of subject, then I'm going home. You've spent a lot of time in Canada. It was once a British colony, right?"

"I guess. That was before my time."

"If you had something that mentioned 'B. Park,' what would it be referring to? Something maybe important to Queen Elizabeth."

"I don't know, Bud," Shorty said. "Except maybe Bletchley Park, which is famous. The work done there was said to have ended World War II at least two years early and saved several million lives."

"Bletchley Park? Never heard of it. In Canada?"

"I'm not surprised. It was top secret in England until the British government finally acknowledged it in 2009. Most relatives of the people who worked there never knew anything except that some kind of secret war work was done. It was where they broke the German war codes. But I need to run. I told Callie I'd get some groceries for dinner. "

"Me, too," Bud replied. "I'm going to surprise Wilma Jean with dinner and get takeout from the cafe. I did that last night and it was a big success, though she probably won't be around to enjoy it, as she and Maureen are catering a big anniversary party."

Shorty laughed as he headed out the door, Bud close behind, thinking of how it was good to be back in Green River, and how he looked forward to a quiet evening with the dogs and a good book.

Maybe he'd finally find time to start that one Wilma Jean had brought home—what was it called? *The Ice House Cafe?* She had said it had some interesting parts, especially about zombies. He wasn't real big on zombies, but her recommendation held a lot of weight, especially since she was on the Green River Library Board of Directors.

He locked the office door and headed for the bungalow, no idea that the events to come would make dealing with zombies seem like a picnic.

26

Bud sat on the back deck of the bungalow watching the sunset, the dogs at his feet, begging for bites of beef stew. He'd stopped by the cafe for takeout, but for some reason, it wasn't as tasty as usual, probably because he knew his wife hadn't cooked it, having been busy preparing the anniversary dinner.

He thought about what Shorty had said about how unlikely it was for a dire bear to be on the plateau, which made him feel better, though he still wondered what exactly was up there. Whatever it was, it made him appreciate being in the pastoral setting of Green River, which in turn made him wonder how the melon harvest was going.

He knew Kale would contact him if there were any problems, so he figured all was going well, though he thought that maybe he should drive on out there and check things out anyway. It was late enough in the day that the odds of Kale conscripting him for some task were small.

He took the note from his pocket with the Morse code and Howie's translation, reading it again:

COUSIN ELIZ YR WRK AT B. PK NVR FRGTN PRINC ELIZ

He decided it was meant to read, *Cousin Elizabeth your work at B. Park never forgotten, Princess Elizabeth.*

Shorty had guessed that B. Park stood for Bletchley Park, which was where the German war codes were translated, some place in England, with Princess Elizabeth somehow involved.

He stood and went back into the house, dogs at his heels, the sun having disappeared into a golden glow behind the distant San Rafael Swell. Sitting in his recliner, he opened his laptop and began a search on Bletchley Park.

Bletchley Park is an English estate in Bletchley, Buckinhamshire that became the principal centre of Allied code-breaking during World War II. The team at Bletchley Park devised automatic machinery to help with decryption of the German Enigma machine, culminating in the development of the world's first computer under the direction of Alan Turing. Code-breaking operations at Bletchley Park ended in 1946, and all information about the wartime operations was classified until the British government declassified the information in July, 2009, finally acknowledging the contribution of the many people working there.

After the War, the secrecy imposed on Bletchley staff remained in force, so that most relatives never knew more than that a child, spouse, or parent had done some kind of secret war work. Everyone who came to Bletchley was required to sign the Official Secrets Act, in which they agreed not to disclose anything about their work at Bletchley, with severe legal penalties.

About three-quarters of the code-breakers there were women, many who held degrees in mathematics, physics, and engineering. They performed calculations and coding and hence were integral to the computing processes. Bletchley's work was essential to many Allied successes, including defeating the U-boats in the Battle of the Atlantic and success at D-Day in June of 1944, when the Allies knew the locations of all but two of Germany's fifty-eight Western-front divisions.

Bud found this all very interesting, and it made sense that none of these code-breakers were acknowledged, given the necessary secrecy. Was that the reason for the mittens? The code-breakers could be recognized in a subtle and secret way with a Morse code message, but why by Princess Elizabeth?

He continued his Internet search.

Queen Elizabeth II and her sister, Princess Margaret, were known to knit socks for soldiers during World War II. Both were photographed knitting during the war effort, a symbol of their support for the troops. During World War I and World War II, ordinary women all over Europe were recruited as spies for both sides. As knitting was common at the time, a woman at a window with a pair of needles and a ball of yarn was inconspicuous. They observed the comings and goings of soldiers and other important strategists, and since knitting's binary stitch system translates easily into code, they could secretly embed information into their projects.

Bud thought of Cy wanting the mittens, and wondered if he'd gotten a motel room in Price. Had Christian come back? Bud could see him returning to get his pickup, but it seemed like the fancy dance would be a lost cause, now that his costume was destroyed.

Bud sighed, hoping they would all go back to Salt Lake, though he somehow suspected Cy wasn't going anywhere until he finished his self-imposed mission of finding the Grandfathers, assuming that in itself wasn't a fabrication. One had to admire the guy for his tenacity, Bud thought, pushing the recliner footrest back.

He sat up, again remembering one last thing he wanted to look into. He'd had a hunch ever since Howie had told him the story about the woman on the radio up at Scofield Reservoir, and he wanted to check it out.

He searched on *Scofield Utah radio*. He was surprised at how quickly his search was productive, probably because there weren't many entries for Scofield. The date on the article was about the same as when Howie had gotten out of high school.

He read:

The FCC Enforcement Bureau has affirmed an $8,500 fine each against Sarah and Brian Crow of Scofield, Utah for deliberately interfering with

Amateur Radio communications. The FCC said it imposed the financial penalty because of the couple's "willful and repeated violation" of Section 333 of the Communications Act and of Sections 97.101(d) and 97.119(a) of the Amateur Service rules by causing intentional interference to licensed radio operations by deceiving other radio operators and by failing to transmit their assigned call signs.

The FCC said the evidence indicated that the transmissions at issue were aimed at misleading other radio amateurs into believing they were communicating with an actual person, when it was in fact a recording. This is considered to be broadcasting, which is illegal on amateur frequencies. At other times, Sarah Crow would actually talk to the radio amateur, making them believe she was a distraught woman from the past. They admitted to doing this for "entertainment."

Commission agents used radio direction-finding techniques to pin down the transmission sources. FCC agents monitored transmissions from the couple's station for approximately three hours on June 14 and heard them transmit "a voice transmission of a supposedly deceased woman on 14.313 MHz."

These transmissions prevented other amateur licensees from communicating over the frequency, and neither of the couple transmitted their assigned call signs while the agents were listening.

The FCC agents visited the couple's residence and asked to inspect their station, which they confirmed was capable of operating on 14.313 MHz, the frequency they always used. In addition to the fines, their equipment was confiscated.

Bud closed his computer, leaning back. He'd been right after all— it was a hoax, one that poor Howie had fallen for, though he was admittedly only a teenager. It was sad, though, that it had resulted in taking the enjoyment of the hobby from him.

Bud now felt like it had been a productive evening, and he'd share what he'd found with Howie next time he saw him. Actually, he thought, maybe he should share it now, for he knew Howie was working at the drive-in, and his stomach told him the beef stew wasn't going to hold him much longer, especially since he'd fed most of it to the dogs.

He'd head on down there and check out Chance's mural while having a BBQ sandwich.

He gave Hoppie and Pierre their obligatory biscuits, then loaded Lindie into his FJ, thinking he'd leave the two little dogs to hold down the fort until Wilma Jean got home. That way, if he decided to stop by the farm and help out, they wouldn't have to sit in his FJ.

Lindie was always good, but the other two were experts at finding mischief, especially little Pierre, who hated tractors and tried to bite their tires, earning him the nickname on the farm of *Pierre Tirebiter*.

He then went back inside and turned on the kitchen light, thinking that, since it was almost dark, they wouldn't worry as much until he or Wilma Jean got home.

He pulled out of the drive, Lindie happily watching from the passenger seat, neither having any idea that they wouldn't be coming home for what would seem like a long time.

27

Even in the waning light, Bud could fully appreciate Chance's mural, along with a small crowd who was taking photos and admiring it.

He'd been right about it being a radio tower, and Chance had added two more rays emanating from it, one ending in a giant cinnamon roll, and the other in an ice-cream cone. In the center of the tower was Howie's call sign, WØRQC, and beneath it all, in bubble letters with beveled edges, were the words *Blue Moon*.

Nowhere to be seen, Bud figured Chance was probably relaxing in what he must consider pretty fancy digs—Howie's barn. Howie was inside the drive-in, serving ice-cream cones to a line of kids as the neon sign announcing *Howie's Drive-In* began flickering in the fading daylight.

Bud had just finished his BBQ sandwich and was contemplating going inside and getting in the ice-cream line when a tall thin man with black hair in a ponytail walked up.

"Mind if I share your table?" he asked, the others all being taken.

"Have a seat," Bud replied. "I'm about done, anyway."

"Don't leave on my behalf," the man said, holding out his hand, though he struck Bud as being a bit stand-offish. "Earl Walker."

"Nice to meet you, Earl," Bud replied, shaking hands. "Bud Shumway."

"Not Sheriff Bud Shumway?" Earl said in surprise.

Bud noted that he seemed taken aback, though he tried to hide it. He had an air of familiarity about him that Bud couldn't quite place.

"One and the same," Bud said.

"Are you eating out while on duty?" Earl asked.

"Small-town sheriffs are always on duty," Bud replied, smiling. "But technically I'm off for the day. Are you wanting to report something?"

"Nah, just making small talk," Earl said. "Do they come take your order, or do you have to go inside?"

"You have to go inside," Bud replied. "Try the BBQ. It's delicious."

"Thanks," Earl replied, standing.

As he walked away, Bud realized why the man seemed familiar— he reminded him of Christian, even down to the pony tail.

They must be related, Bud mused. He'd ask when the guy came back out. He could see that a table inside had opened up, and after Earl ordered, he sat down at one. Bud noted that he seemed to be in a bad mood.

Not wanting to be intrusive, Bud instead went to his FJ, where Lindie waited. He would take her out for a short walk, as it was a nice balmy evening, too nice to go home, especially since his wife wouldn't be there.

He turned toward the ball fields at the edge of town, then remembering that they were getting infested with goatheads, which were particularly hard on dog paws, he instead decided to go the other direction out by Old Man Green's farm, where there were some empty fields they could walk around near an irrigation ditch. He knew he should go on out to his own farm and see how the harvest was coming, but it was late, and he knew everything would be buttoned up for the night.

He pulled over by one of the fields and let Lindie out, then decided to call Kale and see how things were going, dialing the number as Lindie dipped into the water.

"Hello," Kale answered. "How's everything going, Bud?"

"I'm calling to ask you that same question," Bud replied. "Are you guys making any headway?"

"We just finished that field of honeydews. We'll be done in a couple of days at this rate. Stop by when you get a chance, though I know you're busy."

"Busy?" Bud asked absentmindedly, fishing in his pocket for his harmonica. "Has Molly been busy out at the B&B?"

"Things have quieted down a bit," Kale replied. "Which is good, as she was getting pretty stressed." He paused, then said, "Bud, we're both going to take some time off after the harvest. Wilma Jean said that was fine by her regarding the B&B. You OK with that as far as the farm goes?"

"Sure," Bud said. "I thought we had a standing agreement that you can take as much time as you want when the harvest is done. Go visit the kids."

"Molly wants to go back to Ireland for a couple of weeks."

"Ireland? That sounds fantastic."

Now pulling the harmonica from his pocket, Bud asked, "Say, do you by any chance know the words to that old song, *Summertime*?"

"What?"

"*Summertime*."

Kale replied, "About all I know is, *The livin' is easy, fish are jumpin' and the cotton is high*. Why do you ask?"

"I'm trying to learn it on the harmonica."

"Why do you need the words if you're playing the harmonica?"

"I don't know. It helps me remember the tune. You need me for anything out there?"

Kale replied, "Bud, I know how hard you worked, trying to run this place by yourself before I came on board. Don't worry about anything. I've got plenty of help, and you have other things to take care of. You know I'll call if I need anything."

"I appreciate that, Kale," Bud replied. "It's nice to know everything's in good hands."

They said goodbye just in time for Bud's phone to ring.

"Yell-ow."

"Is this Sheriff Shumway?"

"It is," Bud replied. "What can I do for you?"

"Bud, this is Auggie. You remember me and Maddie? Well, we really need your help. I'm sitting in the parking lot at the grocery store in Castle Dale. Can you come over right away?"

The tone of Auggie's voice immediately left Bud with an ominous feeling.

"What's going on, Auggie?"

"Bud, we were both over at the cave excavating, and Maddie said she wasn't feeling well. I think she was dehydrated, because it was getting hot, and she won't drink like she should. Anyway, she left to go back to the Orange Olsen house, and I was maybe an hour behind her. But when I got there, she was gone, no sign of her anywhere."

"Was the van still there?" Bud asked.

"It was," Auggie replied. "But what was bad was that when I opened the door to go inside the house, well, Sheriff, I can't even begin to describe it."

There was a long pause, until Bud finally asked, "Can you try?"

"Oh, sorry," Auggie said, sounding like he was going to cry. "The place was basically destroyed, and I mean destroyed. Stuff strewn everywhere as if someone had just flung it all around. Things ripped up, torn up, wrecked, mangled, demolished, pulverized, obliterated, disintegrated, and smashed. It was horrible."

"You're doing a good job describing it," Bud said. "But what about Maddie?"

"Like I said, she's gone. Totally gone. No hide nor hair of her. Sheriff, please come over. I have no idea what to do."

"I'm not sure what I can do in the dark, Auggie," Bud said. "Do you have a place you can go for the night?"

"I want to go back and wait there in case she shows back up. She could be injured."

"Maybe not a good idea to be there alone, Auggie," Bud said. "Like I said, I'm not sure what I can do until morning, but I guess I'll come on over and see if I can be of any help. Maddie missing is definitely a worry. Any clues as to what might have happened?"

"Not really," Auggie said, now sounding more hopeful. "Probably that bear. I'm going to spend the night in the van."

"What bear?" Bud asked.

"You know, the bear that's been making trouble everywhere on the plateau. The one that injured that sheepherder."

"OK," Bud said. "I may end up going to Price for the night afterwards, depending on what we find. Might be a good idea for you to wait for me and not go back alone."

"Sounds good to me," Auggie replied. "I'll wait here at the grocery store parking lot. How long?"

"Probably at least an hour, Auggie, maybe even a little longer."

"OK, I'll get some groceries while I wait. And Bud, I forgot one thing. This afternoon, we had a visitor, a guy with a pony tail, a native-looking guy. He came and asked some questions about what we were doing, investigation type stuff, and neither of us felt comfortable, so we pretty much asked him to leave, though in a nice way. We just told him we needed to get back to work."

"Do you think he destroyed your stuff?"

"I don't know, but if he did, he needs therapy. We were nice to the guy, no reason to go all feral on us."

"I suspect the answer is in that very word, Auggie," Bud said.

"What word?"

"Feral. See you soon."

With that, Bud hung up and gathered up Lindie, wondering why a bear would destroy the Orange Olsen house. And hadn't Auggie said he'd opened the door when he got back?

The bear was not only destructive, Bud mused, but was polite enough to close the door behind it after it was done.

28

After hanging up with Auggie, Bud dialed the drive-in.

"Howie, I'm on my way over to Castle Dale. Could you make sure Wilma Jean knows? I tried to leave her a message, but I'm not sure she'll get it, she's so busy."

"Sure, not a problem, but do you mind me asking why?"

"Well," Bud replied. "Because I want her to know I won't be home until late tonight."

"No, Sheriff, I mean, why are you going to Castle Dale this late in the day?"

"I just got a call from Auggie. He's in Castle Dale. Someone or something trashed their house, and Maddie's missing."

"That's terrible, Bud," Howie replied. "Say, I'm getting ready to close up here. Would you like some company? Maureen's busy helping your wife, so I'm batching it, too."

"Where's little Mal?" Bud asked.

"His grandma has him. I'll call her and have her make sure our wives know what's going on. Swing by the drive-in. I'll have it closed up by the time you get here." Howie paused, then added, "Uh, oh, here comes Chance. Chances are good he'll want to come, too."

Bud replied, "The more the merrier, as long as he knows we probably won't be back until late."

"What do you think of the mural he did?" Howie asked.

"It's fantastic," Bud replied. "It's definitely gonna put Green River on the map. I'm almost there if you're sure you want to go."

"I just turned out the lights, so I'll be waiting."

As Bud pulled up to the drive-in, he could see Howie and Chance both waiting outside. Chance came to the FJ window and asked, "Can I hitch a ride with you, Mr. Shumway? I got word that my dad's getting older, and I want to go see him."

Bud replied, "Well, sure, but Castle Dale is the wrong direction from Detroit, and it doesn't have any trains."

"No, I'm wanting to go to Reno," Chance replied. "That's where he lives. How close would the nearest train be from where you're going?"

Howie said, "You'd want to go to Helper, which is a good 25 or 30 miles away. That's where the station is."

"Is Castle Dale on the highway?" Chance asked.

"Most towns are," Howie said.

"I've been to a few that weren't," Chance replied. "I'd just get on a train here in Green River, but the only one that stops is Amtrak. But I could go with you guys and then hitch a ride up to Helper. Do the trains stop there?"

"If you mean freight trains, yes, they stop," Bud replied. "That's where they add on helper engines to get them over Soldier Summit. You're welcome to go with us to Castle Dale, though you're going to have trouble hitching at night."

"Is it illegal?" Chance asked. "If so, I can just sleep in the bushes and hitch a ride the next day."

"What difference does it make what time you hitch if it's illegal?" Howie asked.

"I won't have the sheriff around to notice tomorrow," Chance said, giving him an exasperated look.

"What happened to painting Howie's caboose and the windows around town, or is your dad that urgent?" Bud asked.

Chance replied, "Well, Howie paid me for doing his drive-in, and now that I have some cash, I just feel like I need to go see my dad. I haven't seen him for a couple of years."

They got into the FJ, Howie sliding into the back with Lindie, asking, "Where's Hoppie and the weens?"

"They stayed home," Bud replied. "They're better off there chewing on bones until Wilma Jean gets home."

"What's a weens?" Chance asked. "Is that a band or something, Hoppie and the Weens?"

"Wiener dog," Howie replied.

"Oh, a weens. They're scary little buggers," Chance said as they headed toward the freeway.

"I'm going to go the long way and stay on the freeway instead of taking the cutoff, since it's getting dark," Bud said. "I think it'll end up taking about the same amount of time or maybe even be a little quicker, as the drive's easier in the dark, no bumps and potholes."

Howie said to Chance, "It's the scenic way across the Swell."

It was completely dark by the time they crossed the long sweep between Green River and the Hanksville exit, and as they reached the road to Black Dragon Canyon, Howie pointed to it, saying, "There's the road to Black Dragon. There's some nice petroglyphs there."

"Nice," Chance said from the front passenger seat, looking out the window, though Bud knew he couldn't see anything.

Finally topping the Swell, Howie said, "If you look back, you'll see the incredible cliffs where the highway was blasted through Spotted Wolf Canyon."

Chance turned, looking back into the darkness, saying again, "Nice."

Howie continued pointing out landmarks as Bud drove through the night.

"There's Dutchman Arch. It's called that because it's kind of shaped like a wooden shoe."

"Nice."

"Swasey's Cabin."

"Nice."

"Those pinnacles are called Joe and his Dog."

"Fantastic."

"Sid's Leap is over there. That's where this guy jumped his horse across a twelve-foot wide crevasse."

"Crazy."

"Ghost Rock."

"Spooky."

"We're now crossing Eagle Canyon. A base jumper tried to jump off the bridge here once but he'd misjudged the depth and crashed. Fortunately, he survived."

"Not too bright."

"Way over there's a nice dinosaur track. Probably a therapod."

"Interesting."

"There's a huge stand of Fremont mahonia over in those cliffs. Also called desert holly."

"Sounds nice, whatever that is."

"Finally, as they dropped down the other side of the Swell, Howie said, "We're leaving the freeway now and taking the Moore Cutoff over to Highway 10, which will take us along Castle Valley on the back side of the Swell."

"Swell."

They had soon gone through the small farming town of Ferron and were in Castle Dale, pulling up in front of Stewart's Marketplace. Bud noted there was no white van.

Waiting for awhile, he finally said, "Auggie must've gone on back to camp so he'd be there in case Maddie showed up. Let's go on up there. Chance, do you want us to let you out at the edge of town?"

"Why would I want that?" Chance asked.

"I thought you were going to hitch to Helper," Bud replied.

"I'll stay with you guys," Chance replied, looking out the window. "Howie's a good tour guide. I wouldn't want to miss anything. Where exactly are we going?"

"We're going up to Joe's Valley," Howie said. "To investigate bear play."

"What's that?" Chance asked.

"We think a bear tore up a house, and there's a missing person," Howie replied. "We may be getting involved in a search and rescue."

"In the dark?" Chance asked.

"Maybe," Howie replied, looking at Bud.

"Maybe two missing persons," Bud replied. "Unless Auggie's at the house."

"Man, maybe I should get out here if this missing person thing is a trend," Chance replied. "No one would miss me if I went missing."

They started up the road to Joe's Valley, Bud recalling he and Shorty's strange intuitions while on the plateau searching for Cy. It seemed there was indeed a bear running amok, and if it was the same one that had harmed the sheepherder, it was definitely dangerous.

He hoped that Auggie and Maddie were both waiting at the Orange Olsen house instead of an angry bear, a bear possibly wearing a radio collar.

He knew they'd find out soon enough as he finally reached Joe's Valley, the black outline of the reservoir hugging the road.

29

"This spaghetti is delicious," Bud said, scooping the last of it from a paper bowl with a plastic fork. "And the garlic bread is, too. Another win for the Dire Bear Cafe."

They'd found Auggie at the Orange Olsen house, cooking dinner in the midst of the chaos, having cleared enough room on the countertops to make spaghetti, garlic bread, and a tossed salad, along with frog-eye salad from the grocery deli. Bud and Howie had set the table back upright from where it had been turned on its top so they could sit there to eat.

"I'll do the dishes," Howie said, picking up everyone's paper plates and putting them in a trash bag. "Bud, we should probably take this trash back with us so we don't attract another bear."

Looking around, Bud said, "Do you really think a bear did this, Auggie? It isn't as bad as I expected it to be."

Auggie replied, "I was sure of it at first, but now that we're back here looking around I'm not so sure. My first impression was the place was trashed, but either someone came in and cleaned it up, or I was being hysterical. It doesn't make sense that someone would come back and pick things up, so I guess I was being hysterical."

"It's bad enough, Sheriff," Howie said glumly. "We need to help Auggie clean it all up."

"Agreed," Bud said. "But let's let Chance and Auggie do it while we go look for Maddie. We need to find her ASAP."

Bud looked around cursorily as he talked, distracted, then asked, "Auggie, can you tell if Maddie took anything with her, like her coat or that kind of thing? Is it possible she left before the house was trashed?"

Looking around, Auggie replied, "Actually, Sheriff, her coat is missing, as well as her hiking boots. And it looks like she took a small backpack that has her GPS and camera. It's like she was going somewhere as opposed to just fleeing mindlessly."

"So," Bud mused. "She probably did leave before the bear came in. And she never said anything to you about going somewhere?"

"No, but I know she was upset from that guy who came in and acted like he was interrogating us."

"Do you think she's running away from something?" Bud asked. "Maybe this place wasn't really torn up by a bear, and it was a diversionary tactic as an excuse for her to get away."

Auggie looked disturbed. "I wouldn't go that far—I mean that's like a conspiracy theory. Why would she want to do that?"

"Maybe someone's looking for her," Bud said. "Maybe it's the guy with the ponytail. If it looked like a bear had torn things up, it would give her a good excuse to go missing. What kind of questions was he asking?"

"Well, he started out asking just sort of general stuff like you would do if you were making casual conversation, like where we're from, what we're doing, kind of just general talk, and then he started asking about bears. He pretended that he was just casually interested, but it seemed suspicious. At that point, I didn't want to talk to him any more."

"Why not? And why will you talk to me and not to him?" Bud asked.

"Because I know you're the sheriff, and I didn't know who that guy was. And I don't want to talk about bears, seeing what's been going on."

"Did he tell you his name?"

"Yeah, it was Earl Walker."

"When was he here?"

"Earlier in the day."

"Did you tell him you were working on dire bears?"

"No we never even mentioned it. We just told him we were doing some basic geology stuff. In a way we kind of are. You have to know geology to understand the paleontology."

Howie said, "Sheriff, I think a bear did this. I don't see a human having any desire to wreck things like this. It's unusual for a bear to break into an actual house, but when they do, they usually just look for food, they don't destroy everything. It's like it's mad at somebody."

"This is scary," Chance said. "A bear's bad enough, but a *mad* bear?"

Howie continued. "Shorty told me about a bear up in the Yukon that totally destroyed a hunting camp because it was mad at hunters."

"I'm terrified that bear could be out there, especially with Maddie on foot," Auggie said.

"Do you guys have bear spray?" Bud asked.

"We each carry a canister. I assume Maddie has hers with her."

As they talked, Bud walked around the house, examining things. Picking up what appeared to be a set of goggles, he asked, "What do you use these for?"

Auggie replied, "They're goggles. They belong to Maddie."

"She plays some kind of video games up here?"

Auggie sighed. "Look, Sheriff, Maddie and I are not the best of friends. We don't make very good working partners and are here together only because we both have students that need to do their capstone fieldwork next semester, so we're here getting this dig site ready to go. If I'd known what I know about her now, I wouldn't have come out with her. She's a good teacher and paleontologist, but her ideas and mine are worlds apart."

"How so?" Bud asked.

"She wants to reintroduce the Pleistocene animals, and I don't think it can be done, and even if it can I'm not sure it's a good idea. We've had lots of arguments about it. She thinks this dig will result in a complete dire-bear genome."

"That doesn't sound like something that would cause a huge rift," Bud said.

"There's more, but I don't really want to talk about it. I don't know much about it anyway, because she won't talk to me."

"Back to the goggles," Bud said. "Do they have something to do with all this?"

"Have you ever heard of FPV drones?" Auggie asked.

"I have," Howie replied. "I actually own a drone, but it's not an FPV. You need a ham license to operate them, and I just recently got my ticket—that's what hams call their license. FPV stands for First Person View. You can see where the drone is as if you were in it, like in an airplane. It flies on ham frequencies, is why you need a ham license."

"So Maddie has an FPV drone?" Bud asked.

"No," Auggie replied. "But it's like that. She can see what's going on, and even transmit sound through it."

"But it's some kind of drone," Bud said. "What else could it be? It has to carry a transmitter/receiver for her to do all that."

"A transceiver, Bud," Howie corrected.

"Auggie," Bud said patiently. "There's something going on here, and you need to be straightforward with us. We need to know—especially since Maddie's now missing. We need to know exactly what we're dealing with. What are the goggles for? Some kind of radio collar?"

Auggie sighed. "Well, at least she can't accuse me of telling you, since you guessed it. Yes, a radio collar. There's a bear on the loose, and it has a radio collar with a camera on it so she can track it."

"So this is how she knew about the sheepherder being injured," Bud said. "There was no other way than being there, because it just happened recently and in a different county. And how exactly did she save the sheepherder? By playing music? She was watching it all come down with her goggles?"

"Exactly," Auggie said.

"This is all really wild," Chance said.

"What's the story of the bear?" Bud asked.

"Apparently it's part of a project to study bears in foreign habitats and how they adapt. It has nothing to do with this dig, except to reinforce her beliefs that dire bears can be brought back. She's working with some wildlife biologists, or so she says. I don't know where they brought this bear from. That's all I know about it."

"Is it the same bear that's terrorizing people?" Howie asked.

Auggie replied, "I really don't know, but I would suspect it is."

"Have you ever seen it?" Bud asked.

"No, and I don't want to. I'm going to leave as soon as Maddie's found. I'm done."

"Auggie, we need to get going, but could you show me how to use the goggles? Actually, show Howie, as he's better at stuff like that."

"Sure."

Auggie first turned on the goggles, then placed them on Howie's face.

"I can see something," Howie whispered dramatically. "It looks like the window of a house with people inside talking—I'm hiding in the bushes, and I'm really really big."

Howie took off the goggles, adding, "Just kidding."

Chance said, "I'm never going out that door again. Can I spend the night in here?"

"I was going to recommend that," Bud said. "We're going to drive up the plateau as far as we can, then probably head to Price and come back in the morning. It would be good if you stayed here with Auggie in case he needed your help."

"We can sleep in the van," Auggie said. "As long as you don't snore."

"I never snore when I'm scared, because I don't sleep," Chance replied.

"I'm going to take these goggles with us," Bud said as he and Howie headed out the door, Lindie close behind.

Even though Bud knew they couldn't search very effectively in the dark, he felt that they had to try, and he knew it would be a long night, regardless, for he was already tired, and even though they would go to the house in Price, it was still a long ways.

It would give him plenty of time to wonder if Earl Walker was the same Earl he'd heard mentioned while listening to the fox hunters talking on Christian's radio ages ago in Tusher Canyon—and to also wonder if Christian and Cy had come back and were maybe even on the plateau that very moment.

30

The road climbing from the Orange Olsen house seemed steeper than usual, but Bud knew it was just the effect of not being able to see the landscape around them. The nights were already starting to get longer with autumn, and he knew there would soon be a time when one couldn't even drive the road, for it would sleep under deep snows.

"Kind of spooky up here at night, especially thinking about some bear running wild," Howie commented. "Kind of reminds me of that time up at Scofield Reservoir when I heard that voice from the past."

"I have something to tell you about that," Bud said, but Howie continued talking, not seeming to hear him.

"I'm going to invent a radio called a Speak Easy, Bud. But I've been thinking about Scofield a lot since I got back into all this, and I'm wondering if it might've been an SDE or LDE, though neither really explains it."

Sensing Howie was nervous, Bud decided to just let him talk. He asked, "What are those?"

"Well, an SDE is a short-delayed echo and an LDE is a long-delayed echo, or anything 2.7 seconds later. Sometimes you'll hear your signal repeated after a few moments. It's kind of eerie until you realize what it is. There are lots of theories about it, but nobody knows what actually causes it."

"What are the theories?"

"Reflections in outer space or reflections within the Earth's magnetosphere. Some think a delayed echo is a signal caught along a magnetic field line of the Earth. Signals can travel around the Earth seven times in one second. The most popular theory is that the radio signals are trapped between two ionized layers in the atmosphere and are guided around the world many times until they fall out of a gap in the bottom layer. There are other theories, and they get really technical, and some even think it's a moon bounce."

"So, you could have a delay of one-hundred years, like the voice of that woman at Scofield?" Bud asked.

Howie replied, "No, that's why that was probably something else. Electromagnetic waves aren't fully understood. They're one of the four things physicists think are critical to how the universe works, along with gravity and a couple of quantum physics things that I don't understand. Most of the universe interacts with radio in one way or another, and hams have access to unbelievable wonders of nature that very few non-hams can even dream of. It's a vast unexplored playground."

Bud replied, "Like I said, it's magic, Howie, and you're like a wizard."

Howie replied, "It's the closest thing to magic one will ever get their hands on. What excites me about radio is that it's a natural phenomenon. We can generate this invisible signal and throw it out there with voices and images on it."

Bud geared down, slowing.

"That whole conversation up at Scofield was a hoax, Howie. I can prove it when we get back. I found an article on the Internet where these people in Scofield were fined for hoaxing people. The date matches when you were up there."

Howie turned to look at Bud, his profile outlined by stars through the window.

"No kidding?"

"For real."

"I gave up ham radio for a hoax?"

"There was no way you could've known. They were fined a lot for that time."

"How much?"

"Eight thousand and change each."

"That's a lot even for now. They must've been hoaxing a lot of people."

Bud asked, "Any idea how we're going to find Maddie in the dark, especially if she's not walking down the road?"

"I don't know, but I sure wouldn't want to be alone out here at night," Howie replied. "Well, better alone than with a bear, I guess."

"We're on top now," Bud said. "Let's get out and yell and see if anyone answers."

"Would she have had time to get up here by now?"

"I think so. It's not that far."

They got out of the FJ, Bud making Lindie stay as they began yelling into the night.

"Helloooo, anybody out there?"

It wasn't long before they were back inside the FJ.

"No echoes up here," Howie said. "It's spooky. Sheriff, tell me this. Humans can go to the moon, go into the deepest oceans, build incredible things, yet we're still afraid of the dark."

"It's because we can't see. We're creatures of the light."

"I like that. Creatures of the light. Sounds like a sci-fi film—a not very scary one."

They sat in the dark for awhile, silent, until Howie said, "Do you think Chance will go to Reno?"

"I don't know. I hope he does something to find his way in life. He's a talented artist," Bud said.

"I hope so, too," Howie replied. "He kind of reminds me of myself."

"How so?"

"I was pretty lost at sea when I was his age. You know, Bud, I've never told anyone this story, but maybe it will help explain things a little, I don't know. But there was a time in my life when I was feeling pretty hopeless. I was renting a little shack in Sunnyside and couldn't find a job and didn't even have a car—this was before I met Maureen and started the drive-in. I was pretty young and had a lot to figure out, but one night, all alone and lonely, I decided that I would hitch out to the Pacific Ocean and walk into the water and just keep walking. That way, nobody would have to deal with anything, I'd just go missing. Plus I'd never seen the ocean, and I'd get to see it before I died."

"Gee, that's awful, Howie. I'm glad you didn't go through with it."

"Well, I tried. I started hitching and eventually got a ride. I don't know if you've ever hitchhiked, Bud, but in general, bad people don't bother you, unless it's to yell at you or something. Nice people pick you up because they're the ones who care about some stranger standing by the road. Keep in mind that this was back awhile ago before people got so paranoid."

"But what happened?" Bud asked.

"Well, by the time I reached Nevada, I was feeling better. See, when you ride with a stranger, you know it's only a short time until you reach a fork in the road and part ways, so you can be perfectly honest with each other. You can also be honest with yourself. So you can learn a lot from them and yourself both. But it was my guitar that saved me."

"How so?"

"I think people gave me a ride because they saw it and figured I was just some sensitive lost musician, which I kind of am. They knew I didn't have any money or I wouldn't be hitching, and money doesn't mean much in that situation anyway. So as I went along, hitching my way through Nevada and then California, I started to find some confidence in myself and the world in general. By the time I reached the ocean, I was changed."

He paused for a moment, thinking, then continued. "I camped in the redwoods for awhile, and I realized that I was free. The fear and uncertainty of hitching was worth seeing the stars at night and sitting under the big trees. I was seeing things I hadn't seen before, and it changed me. And I finally realized I had to come back and be responsible for myself, which I did, but sometimes I really miss that feeling of freedom."

"I understand completely," Bud said. "I think that a lot of us have felt that way at one time or another, and for me, it's how I feel when I'm juoksentelisinkohan."

"What's that?"

"It's Finnish for wondering if one should wander around aimlessly."

Howie laughed. "That's what little Mal does all the time. His life consists of wandering around aimlessly, but he doesn't stop to wonder if he should do it, he just does it."

Bud laughed. "It's almost as if just saying the word reflects its meaning, it's so long and aimless. But maybe it's about returning to a simpler time, one where we're more like kids."

Howie said, "I'm beginning to think that everything you knew as a kid was truth. I need to stick with that, 'cause it will never let you down."

"I agree," Bud replied. "But Howie, does that look like a fire way over there in the trees? Look just to the right of that big shadow."

"You mean the big shadow that's moving?" Howie asked as Lindie began growling.

"Well, now it would be to its left," Bud said. "Since it's definitely moving."

"And moving toward the fire," Howie said. "Sheriff, that looks like somebody's campfire. We need to get over there fast, before whatever that shadow is does."

"Agreed," Bud said. "But most animals would run from a fire, not head toward it, so I'm wondering what that could be. I remember seeing an old overgrown road taking off back down a ways. Let's try it out."

Bud turned around and they were soon heading on an old road through a long meadow to the edge of the forest, where a pickup was parked near a small campfire with someone sitting by it. What appeared to be the shadow of some kind of large animal stood nearby as if watching, as improbable as it seemed.

As they pulled next to the pickup, the shadow turned and stood between them and the fire, Lindie growling the whole time.

"It's that bear!" Howie whispered. "It's going to go after whoever that is by the fire. Honk your horn, Sheriff."

As Bud honked, the figure by the fire stood just as the shadow began running away.

"That bear has horns," Bud said, watching as the thing veered away and ran into the trees. "Howie, there's only one animal I know of that's not afraid of much of anything, but I didn't know they were up here on the plateau."

"Moose." Howie said. "They're over in the Books, so it makes sense they've migrated over here now."

"Well, let's go see who we about caused to have a heart attack," Bud replied as they got out and walked to where the figure had sat back down by the fire, ignoring them.

"Whoever it is," Howie added, "I don't think they're real happy to see us."

"I sure hope we just found Maddie," Bud replied. "Happy to see us or not."

"That brown pickup with Saskatchewan plates tells me it's someone else," Howie said.

31

"Evening, Cy," Bud said, touching the brim of his felt hat in acknowledgement.

"Are you having a cookout?" Howie asked. "Why are you way out here?"

Cy turned to look at them, then turned away, saying, "I like lonesome places. Places without any people."

"What about Elizabeth and Christian?" Bud asked. "Where are they?"

"They're still in Salt Lake."

"So, you came back down here by yourself, in Elizabeth's pickup, no less," Bud said. "Aren't you worried you'll break down again?"

"I never left in the first place," Cy replied, stirring the fire. "If I break down, it's just how it goes. What are you two doing out here, if I may ask?"

"We saw the fire and thought you might be having a weenie roast," Howie replied. "Just kidding. We're looking for Maddie. Have you seen her?"

"You mean the woman working on that dig? The one Elizabeth stayed with? What would she be doing up here this time of night?"

"So much for you getting a motel in Price, eh?" Bud asked. "Seriously, Cy, haven't you heard there's a big feral bear on the loose around these parts? Probably not a good idea to be camping."

"I'll sleep in the pickup," Cy replied.

Bud sat on a large log, trying to avoid the smoke from the fire, which appeared to be dying out. Everyone was quiet for some time, staring into the embers, until Howie broke the silence by grunting, "Caveman TV. Need more logs."

Bud said, "No, we need to get going and keep looking for Maddie."

"Maddie's fine," Cy said, looking up.

Bud thought he looked even more tired than when they'd found him wandering around after he and Christian got stuck.

"How do you know that?" Bud asked.

"I just know. I'm a Cree elder. We know things."

Bud studied Cy's face, looking for a hint of emotion, but all he saw was lines from years of struggle and work.

"Cy, what's going on?" he asked.

"What do you mean?"

Bud was silent, the coals glowing, the fire almost dead. For some reason, the immensity of the plateau struck him just then, and the isolation and emptiness woven through the forests and long views made him feel small and insignificant.

Finally, Cy said, "Elizabeth says she's going to divorce me. Fifty-eight years of marriage, and she wants a divorce. She could be polite and wait a few more years. She'd get everything I own."

"Do you have a lot?" Howie asked.

"No, most everything is hers."

Bud replied, "Cy, I'm really sorry, but you can't just come up here and disappear."

"Obviously," he replied sarcastically.

Bud decided to try one more time. "How do you know Maddie's OK? Did you see her?"

"Yes, she was walking up the road, and I offered her a ride. She said she was going to stay in some cave for the night. She seemed fine."

"What about the bear?" Howie asked.

"That bear won't bother her, of all people," Cy said. Then, as if he'd said too much, he stood. "I'm going to go back to Salt Lake and talk Elizabeth into taking me back. We're too old to get divorced, and I'm giving up on ever finding the Grandfathers."

"It's none of my business, but does her decision have to do with the mittens?" Bud asked.

"You know good and well it does," Cy replied. "She's still pretty frosted over that."

Howie asked, "Did Maddie say exactly what cave she was going to?"

"Yeah, she said the one they're doing the dig in. She said she's going to spend the night there and then go back to the house."

"Did she say what happened?"

"She said a bear broke in."

"OK, but if you truly think Maddie is OK, there's no point in us driving around in the dark up here. Let's make sure this fire is out and then you can follow us back to Price. I'll get you a motel room. We can have breakfast together and figure out things from there."

"What exactly are you going to figure out? How to keep my wife from leaving me?"

"Maybe," Bud replied. "But one more question. Do you know a guy named Earl Walker?"

"He's my grandson," Cy replied. "How do you know him?"

"He's Christian's brother?"

"No, his cousin. They both live in Salt Lake, but he works for the wildlife people. His mom is my and Elizabeth's daughter. I always thought it was interesting that one grandson worked for the forest service and one worked for the wildlife people, when where I'm from the forest and wildlife pretty much take care of themselves. But then, Saskatchewan's a big place without many people."

"He was over in Green River today," Bud replied.

"What was he doing over there?" Cy asked, then added, "He's way too serious."

"He was having BBQ at Howie's Drive-In, as far as I know. We just said hello is all. But let's get going."

They put out the fire and were soon on their way back down the dusty road, Cy's headlights lighting up the back of the FJ, silhouetting Lindie's ears.

"Howie," Bud said after they'd ridden along in silence for some time. "How did Cy know who Maddie was? As far as I know, he and Christian never stopped at the Dire Bear Cafe when they were going up the plateau and got stuck, and yet he seemed to know who we were talking about."

"And the dig, Bud," Howie added. "He acted like he knew about it. But then, Elizabeth stayed with her, so she probably told him."

"That's true," Bud replied. "But what did he mean when he said the bear wouldn't bother her, of all people? What could that mean?"

"I don't know, Sheriff," Howie replied. "Maybe the bear's afraid of her. Auggie did say she carries bear spray. Maybe it's kind of like Chance is afraid of Wanda."

Bud laughed. "He told you about her trying to get him arrested, eh?"

"He did," Howie answered. "And Auggie said Maddie was part of some kind of study of bears in the wild, how they do in different environments, and they had a radio collar on this one bear, and she's working with some wildlife biologists. Maybe that guy named Earl Walker."

"Cy's grandson and Christian's cousin," Bud replied. "I knew they had to be related from their looks. And Earl fits right into the family with his ham radio stuff."

"What do you mean?" Howie asked.

"I'm pretty sure he was one of the fox hunters out in Tusher Canyon. One of the guys on the radio called another guy Earl. It's not unusual for wildlife guys to also be hunters. A lot of them are attracted to the profession because they like hunting. But anyway, maybe, just maybe, Cy and Christian and even Elizabeth all know about this bear project, along with Earl. Shoots, maybe the whole family's involved."

Howie replied, "That would explain why they were up on the plateau. I wonder if they're getting paid. And I don't blame Auggie for wanting to get away. I would, too."

Howie watched out the window for a bit, then added, "Actually, I'll be glad to get down out of here. These are some of the darkest skies I've ever seen, but I'd be too chicken to sit around up here in the dark with a telescope. But Bud, you're saying it was all a hoax, all the stuff at Scofield? Man, I can't wait to read that report you found."

"We'll be in Price before too long," Bud replied. "We can grab a late dinner, and then you can read to your heart's content. Me and Lindie are going to bed."

"Sounds good," Howie said, looking out the FJ window. "And good old Orion will soon be here to announce it's winter."

"My least favorite constellation," Bud replied as they passed the now dark Dire Bear Cafe, a dim light shining from inside the van.

He added, "I hope those guys sleep well—and also Maddie, wherever she may actually be. And I can't picture telling a stranger where you're going, especially in the dark in a remote area."

"Yup," Howie replied. "Cy has to know Maddie."

32

The crack of a lightning bolt followed by a thunder clap woke Bud, or had it been Lindie, now lying on top of him? He pushed her off, assuring her all was OK.

The glow from the nearby clock read five a.m., and he knew he wouldn't be able to go back to sleep, so he sighed, resigning himself to getting up, as much as he'd like to lounge around.

He normally was up by six anyway, so an hour wouldn't make much difference, he figured. He could make a cup of coffee and go sit out in the back yard, watching the town below wake up from its early autumn sleep.

As Lindie relished her breakfast kibble, Bud thought he could hear Howie fumbling around in the kitchen, and sure enough, he was soon in the back yard, setting a lawn chair next to Bud's.

"You mind if I join you?" Howie asked. "I couldn't sleep."

"Is the bed uncomfortable?" Bud asked. "Wilma Jean said she got a good mattress for the guest bedroom, but she likes them kind of soft."

"No, the bed's comfortable," Howie replied. "I just got to thinking about that deal up at Scofield and got madder and madder. Depriving a kid from an enjoyable hobby, that just wasn't right."

"I read somewhere that ham radio was the King of Hobbies," Bud said. "But I also read it was declining, as fewer people were into it since the advent of things like cell phones and the Internet. But what good does it do being mad about something that happened that many years ago?"

"Delayed anger is better than having it bottled up all your life, Sheriff. Bottling it up leads to things like drinking. But look, speak of the devil, and there it is."

He pointed to the east, where Bud could see an array of stars fading in the dawn's light, a few lingering clouds from the storm drifting on through.

"I'll be darned," he said. "That looks like Orion."

"It is," Howie replied. "It's starting to rise. Orion the Hunter returns, the ghost of the shimmering summer dawn. It's actually visible like this starting in July, but you have to get up before sunrise."

"I had no idea you could see it this time of year," Bud replied.

"It rises on its side, with its three belt stars, Mintaka, Alnitak, and Alnilam, pointing upward. In the winter, it rises in the evening, so you can see it during the night."

"But what's this about it being the ghost of the shimmering summer dawn?" Bud asked.

"That's from a poem by Sophia Prentice, written in 1924. It's quite famous among people of the night."

"As opposed to People of the Light?" Bud laughed.

> Orion, greatest of the tribe,
> That pace the starry heights.
> Ghost of the shimmering summer dawn,
> King of the winter nights!

"That's all I remember. Poetry isn't my thing," Howie said, sipping his coffee. He added, "So, I assume we're going back to Joe's Valley this morning to look for Maddie, as well as check in on Auggie and Chance, assuming they haven't been eaten by a bear."

"I sure hope not," Bud said.

"Sheriff, I had a dream last night, well, during the little stretch of time I did sleep. It was kind of weird."

"What happened?"

"Well, we were sitting in your FJ, up on the plateau, and I was looking through the goggles you got from Auggie."

"I forgot all about those, Howie. They're still in the FJ."

"Well, it was a dream, anyway. I didn't really have the actual goggles," Howie explained patiently.

"Go ahead," Bud said.

"I was looking through the goggles, like I just said, and I was looking out on a big meadow. It was so real, like it was my own eyes."

"Technically, it *was* your eyes," Bud said.

"Don't make me lose my train of thought, Sheriff. Like I said, I need some sleep. But as I stood there, looking around, this guy all dressed in hunting clothes, you know, the kind you buy at Cabella's, came up and saw me and held up his rifle as if to shoot."

"That's quite a dream, Howie. It's as if you were the bear, seeing through its eyes."

"Exactly. But since I had the goggles, I knew I could talk and this guy could hear me. I deduced this from what Auggie said about Maddie playing music when the sheepherder was being mauled, and the bear stopping."

"So you played some music? Did you have your guitar? Did you play something like *Stairway to Heaven*? After all, it was a dream."

"No," Howie replied, sounding frustrated. "I wouldn't be caught dead playing that song, which reminds me, I just wrote a new song called the *CQ Blues*. I'll play it for you sometime."

He paused, then continued, sounding even more frustrated. "I'll tell the story, Bud, if you'll quit interrupting. There was a button on the goggles—is there really a button on them?"

"I don't know."

"Well, I pushed this button and said, 'Don't shoot! I'm harmless.'"

"Did he shoot?" Bud asked.

"No, he just looked shocked. I then said, 'I'm going to turn around now and go back into the forest. Don't shoot. I'll see you later.' I could then see thick foliage, like I was walking back through the forest."

"That's the end of the dream?" Bud asked tentatively.

"That's it."

"No wonder you didn't get any sleep."

"That's not what kept me awake, Bud. I was thinking about everything that's happened lately. I have a question for you."

"Go ahead."

"Cy said he and Christian saw a bear that night when they got stuck. A bear that slammed Christian and bruised his ribs, right?"

"Right."

"But you never found any bear tracks, just three sets of human tracks. So Cy's lying about the bear. He's trying to protect someone, and that someone could very well be Earl, his grandson."

Bud asked, "Why would Earl do that to his own cousin? And I thought we were thinking maybe it was Jack Peroulis, the sheep rancher who's mad at the Forest Service. Maybe he followed them, knowing Christian worked for the Forest Service and wanted to intimidate him, or maybe he just saw the truck and assumed it was someone with the Forest Service."

"But no bear."

"Maybe not."

"So Cy was either lying or mistaken," Howie said.

"Or he did see the bear, but at a different time and place," Bud offered.

"Or the bear came later and tore everything up after they were rescued and before Shorty and I got there the next morning."

"But still no tracks."

"No, but by then everything had pretty much dried up. Hard to leave tracks."

Howie sat silent, the sun now breaking over the distant Tavaputs Plateau, far to the east. Finally, he said, "Sheriff, there's a rogue bear on the plateau, and nobody seems to know anything about it, except Auggie said it was part of an experiment. That means it was brought in from somewhere else. Somebody had to have put that radio collar on it, and I think Maddie was involved. After all, she took off after Earl came and interrogated her and Auggie. That seems suspicious, and I don't think a bear tore up the Orange Olsen house."

"Isn't that pretty much what Auggie told us last night?" Bud asked.

Howie replied, "Have you done any kind of research to see if any bears have gone missing anywhere?"

"No, I never considered putting out an APB for a missing bear. I'm not sure where I would start. But we were talking earlier about Cy and his entire family maybe being involved in all this. I still don't understand why Earl, if it was him, would threaten Christian and maybe even break into his pickup and go through his glove box and vehicle."

"Maybe Earl's not part of the conspiracy."

"Conspiracy?"

"Yes, and it all has something to do with fox hunting and that pair of mittens with the Morse code message and those coordinates you mentioned finding in them. How closely did you examine them, Sheriff? Maybe there's more hidden messages."

"No wonder you didn't get any sleep, Howie," Bud said, suddenly feeling overwhelmed.

"It's a little complicated, isn't it, Sheriff?"

"More than a little," Bud replied. "It's downright convoluted."

"It's being done for money. Somehow, somewhere, there's money involved," Howie said. "It's always that way."

"Money involved in a wild bear terrorizing the plateau?"

"That's the part that kept me up," Howie added. "I can't figure out the motive."

"Could it be money?"

"I know, I know, but figuring out how it all works."

"Count me in with the confused, Howie. But let's get going. We need to find Maddie."

"Are we stopping to get Cy?"

Bud sighed. "I guess so. If we don't, he'll go on back out there and get stuck again or break down. Might as well save ourselves a rescue."

As they picked up the lawn chairs and went inside, Howie said,

"Bud, I have one last question. It's about those mittens and all this complicated Morse code stuff."

"Shoot."

"Why not just use invisible ink? Wouldn't it be a lot easier?"

Bud laughed as they walked out, locking the door behind them while making sure his harmonica was in his pocket.

33

Bud was trying not to huff and puff, more out of pride than anything, as he'd then have to admit his wife was right and he needed to cut back on a few things, like blueberry pie at the cafe.

Lindie was a good dog and had foregone several opportunities to chase squirrels and rabbits, staying dutifully close by, which he figured might be more from the narrowness of the trail than from duty.

As they came around a sharp curve, he could see a declivity ahead, one that looked more like a rock shelter than a cave, with an arched shape where the sandstone had spalled away. He could see it wasn't all that deep, and he thought he could make out someone inside.

He and Howie had met up with Cy earlier, stopping for breakfast burritos at a nearby cafe, along with cups of hot steamy coffee, then taking some to Chance and Auggie at the Dire Bear Cafe.

The pair had been glad to see them, and after some talk, Auggie had described the trail to the cave, where they all suspected Maddie had spent the night. Bud had decided it would be best to go alone, taking only Lindie, in case Maddie was reluctant to talk to anyone.

Howie had put on the goggles, saying he'd keep an eye out in case

Bud ran into the bear, though he was having trouble figuring out the collar's frequency.

Stopping to catch his breath, Bud slipped into the shade of a small juniper tree, then finally stepped into the cave entrance, hoping whoever he'd seen was indeed Maddie. As his eyes got accustomed to the shade, he could see the interior of the cave had several shovels and digging implements leaning against one wall, as well as a grid sectioned off with rope. Maddie was studying something, her back to him.

He said, "Hello Maddie. How's your day going?"

She startled, then said, "You just scared the cheezewhiz out of me. What are you doing here? Where's Auggie?"

Bud replied, "He didn't come, but he told me how to get here. Are you OK?"

"I'm fine," she replied, picking up a shovel. "I'm sorry, but I don't have time to talk. I have a lot to do to get ready for our students."

Bud said, "Well, I'm glad I found you and everything's OK. Wouldn't you like a nice hot meal about now? Auggie's down at the house making some grilled chicken with potato salad and watermelon. It should be ready by the time we get back. We all pitched in and cleaned up the place, so everything's back like it was."

Bud could tell she wanted to go back, yet she replied, "I think I should stay here and work."

He continued. "Maddie, did Auggie tell you he was leaving?"

Looking panicked, she said, "Leaving? He can't leave. I won't have a vehicle if he leaves, and I don't want to be here alone."

"This bear incident really shook him up, Maddie. He's going back to Salt Lake when we leave for Green River. You really should go with him."

"He can't leave me here."

"You can ride to Green River with me, then we can put you on the train to Salt Lake."

"Why would I do that?"

"I don't know, it's just that he said you guys weren't getting along, so I thought maybe that had something to do with why you left last night, and you wouldn't want to ride with him."

"Not getting along? I left because I was afraid of a bear attack. Auggie and I have never really gotten along. He can't ever focus on anything. We have different philosophies, but we do OK, well, OK enough to work together. He can't leave."

"Well Maddie, there's nothing I can do to stop him, and I doubt if there's anything you can do either, so you might as well decide whether you want to go out with us or stay here without a vehicle all alone. I think you'd be wise to go out with us or Auggie."

Maddie sat on a big rock near the cave wall. Bud noted that the rock had deep grooves in it, and asked, "What are these?"

Maddie replied, "They're arrowhead shaft straighteners. Ancient people apparently used this cave, carving these grooves to straighten the wood used to make arrowhead shafts. The shaft was heated up to make it easy to bend, then pressed into one of the grooves. The heat made the shaft more pliable, and placing it in the groove while it cooled made it stay straight. That way they had nice shafts for their spears."

"Interesting," Bud replied. "Maddie, maybe you can help me out here. What song did you play when the bear was mauling the sheepherder?"

"Who told you I played a song? That's ludicrous. How could I do that?"

Bud answered, "It would be pretty easy using the goggles. Auggie told us about the first person view camera on the radio collar. Did you happen to just be watching the bear by chance when all this came down?"

"Auggie talks too much. I was watching, and it's a good thing, too."

"What music did you play?"

"The song *Escape* by Metallica. I have it on my phone."

"Well, there's some irony there," Bud said, then asked, "So, Maddie, exactly why *do* you have a tracker for a radio collar on a bear here on the plateau?"

Maddie sighed. "Auggie can't keep anything to himself. It's just a bear we're watching to see what it does in a strange environment. I'm working with the Utah wildlife people. It's just not a big deal."

"Have you seen anything of interest?"

"No, so far it just seems like a normal bear. It's adapting quite well."

"What kind of bear is it? What was its normal environment like?"

"It's just a big brown bear. It came from the rainforest. Look, Sheriff, there's nothing here that you really need to know. It's a project we'd rather nobody knew about."

"Maddie, this is my jurisdiction. I need to know what's going on here, especially if someone gets injured. But I suppose I could check with the wildlife people and find out more if you don't want to talk to me, they'll tell me if it's all above board and legal. I'll just give them a call later."

Ignoring what Bud had just said, Maddie replied, "I guess if I'm leaving I should get this ready for the winter. Auggie should be here to help. I need to bury the dig so if anybody comes in here they won't see it."

"I can help out," Bud said, picking up a shovel. "Just tell me what to do."

"Does your dog dig? What's her name?"

"Lindie."

"She's sure unusual looking, kind of like a mix between a coyote and a yellow lab."

"She's a Carolina dingo."

As they started throwing dirt on the dig, Bud said, "So, I take it you're going to ride out with Auggie."

"I don't really have a choice, do I? Besides, I'm afraid of that bear."

"Maddie, you and I both know that bear didn't tear up the Orange Olsen house. Who are you trying to fool? Auggie?"

"Are you saying *I* did it? Auggie can be difficult, but he knows about the bear. Why would I tear up our own place?"

"What did Earl want?"

"I don't know."

"Do you think someone was searching for something and that's why they tore up the house?"

"What would they be searching for?"

"Maddie, I noticed the van had a lot of mud on it that night that we came through with Elizabeth. Did you happen to drive up the road before we got there?"

"Why would I want to get stuck?"

Bud sighed, putting down the shovel, as they had finally covered everything up. "I'll ask again—where did this bear came from? You don't just order a big bear and it magically shows up in a UPS truck."

Maddie laughed nervously. "That's almost what happened, kind of. It did come in a truck."

"Who else was involved?" Bud asked, knowing she wouldn't answer. "And why did you slam Christian and break into his pickup?"

"We're good here," she replied. "Grab that shovel and let's go."

"I'll be right behind you," Bud said. "But I want to spend a few minutes here, it's such a special place."

"OK, but watch out for bears," Maddie warned, quickly gone through the trees.

34

Bud stood in the mouth of the shallow cave looking out at the long ridges and valleys of the Wasatch Plateau. It had a familiar feeling, as if he'd spent his childhood there, wandering the countryside exploring, even though he'd actually spent very little time there before the Dire Bear Cafe came to be.

Part of the vast region was in his jurisdiction, but very little involving him ever happened there, as it was so unpopulated. It had its own sense of enchantment, and coupled with a sense of loneliness, he almost felt like he'd somehow tumbled into the past, maybe a good 20,000 years ago or more, during the Great Ice Ages, the time of the Pleistocene megafauna.

He knew the landscape looked very similar to what it had back then, though perhaps with a change of flora and fauna, but the hills and ridges were the same.

And now, in his mind's eye, he began to feel different. He felt much larger and sturdier, with long brown hair and a short pushed-up nose and long fierce teeth. He knew it was his imagination, but he felt like he was turning into a dire bear.

His breathing became heavier, and he had an irresistible urge to claw a nearby tree or turn over a nearby rock. Realizing he was on his hind legs, he dropped to all fours, whereupon he noticed a nearby threat—a yellow dire wolf! It stood looking at a bug on a rock, and he knew it was showing deference by pretending to ignore him, but he knew he had to scare it off anyway.

He began huffing and clacking his teeth, again standing on his hind legs to make himself look bigger, even though he knew he was already huge.

He then started growling—a deep throaty sound that surprised even him at how unnerving it sounded. But instead of scaring the wolf away, it jumped up and lunged at him!

Ready to fight, he soon realized the wolf just wanted to play, for it began tugging on the hair on his ankles while growling and wagging its tail.

Now another bear, a dire bear just like him, except for wearing a very stylish purple radio collar, stood at the cave's entrance. It was huge, and he realized he was just as big, which made him feel proud to be the member of such a special species. But this dire bear was different—along with the radio collar, it was wearing purple mittens.

"I hate secrets," the bear growled. "But if you're going to expose them, you should at least expose them in their entirety, none of this half-baked stuff."

Bud was surprised, but had the sense to ask, "What about the coordinates and MK Tunnels?"

The bear ignored him and kicked at the wolf, who ducked as the bear shuffled away on its hind legs.

Bud sensed something was wrong. A fellow dire bear wearing mittens? Where had it come by mittens, especially ones large enough to fit? And did dire bears actually use words like 'half-baked' while relaying cryptic messages?

On a hunch, he looked down at his arms, and he could see the long sleeves of a denim shirt and someone's tanned hands. And his feet! They were encased in some kind of leather, boots like the humans wore.

He woke. He'd been sitting on the big rock and had somehow slipped down into the soft detritus in the cave and gone to sleep. He quickly jumped up and went outside, still feeling the tension from the dream. Could the rogue bear possibly be nearby? Surely Lindie would notice, but she was busy watching some kind of beetle crawling on a rock, so all must be well.

Turning back to the distant scene, he no longer felt he was turning into a bear, but instead felt a deep sense of sadness. What would it feel like to be the last dire bear, the last of your species, which would then be extinct when you died? You were the last, a creature scientists called an *endling*.

He paused, thinking that it had to be an incredibly lonely feeling, a feeling of desolation, of the end of a time that had stretched out seemingly forever from the beginning, but that was now soon to be over, the end of time for your species with a poignant finality.

But did the last dire bear even realize what was happening? Odds were good they didn't, and their last day was just like any other with no awareness of what was happening on the bigger scale. Did the one they found near the Huntington Mammoth realize that the mammoth was probably its last meal, and with that, the last meal of its entire species? It kind of gave a new meaning to the last supper, Bud thought.

He knew he was standing near where the last known dire bear skeleton had been found, and it was very possible that this was where the endling had lived, even though the species had a wide range. He suspected that nobody realized at that time the species had gone extinct, even though there had undoubtedly been humans around. Or maybe they knew and were glad, as it was such a fearsome creature, and maybe even some human had killed the last one.

It made him feel pensive, and yet, according to Shorty, there had been millions of species gone extinct, and all species were doomed to eventually walk that path. It was just the way of life. He didn't understand it, but he did understand the silent poignancy.

Shorty had mentioned a number of such species, including the last known Mexican grizzly, also called the *oso plateado*, or *silver bear* in Spanish, which was shot in 1976 in Sonora. Many now-extinct species had died at the hands of humans, usually due to hunting for meat or their coats.

As he stood there, he could see the sun's course turning west, and he knew that he needed to get back to the Orange Olsen house and head home.

He thought of Orion, hanging in the sky near the horizon, waiting for winter to make its full appearance, kind of like a dire bear hiding just over the rim of the plateau. He wondered how many species Orion the Hunter had watched go extinct, and he wondered if Maddie would ever manage to clone a dire bear.

Shorty had laughed at the idea, and Bud respected his opinion, but standing out there all alone in such an incredible and uninhabited place, the thought made him shiver.

He then remembered the shaft straightener, and, deciding to look at it more closely, went back inside the shallow cave. Carefully examining the large chunk of sandstone, he wondered how it had come to be inside what was basically a shelter cave.

Someone must have intentionally carried it in there, for there were no signs of it having fallen from the cave's roof. Whoever it was, it must've taken several strong people to carry it, and why would they go to such trouble?

He examined the grooves more closely and realized they had a consistency—all were the same distance apart, like the ribs of an animal. Brushing the dirt away, he realized he was looking at one of Cy's Grandfathers, what he'd described as a ribstone, a petroglyph representing an animal's rib cage.

Looking closer, he found it also had a black painting on its side, apparently done in charcoal—a sketch of an intricate starburst. Hadn't Cy said they'd found the same thing at Swift Current and that this type of drawing was unprecedented in Canadian rock art?

Bud got up, now aware that he was in the presence of more than the dire bear's remains, but also the symbolic remains of an entire culture, likewise unique and irreplaceable. What he was looking at could be the earliest human marking in the Western Hemisphere, made over 18,000 years ago, perhaps after a dire-bear or mammoth hunt.

He paused, the idea somehow feeling heavy and distant. He then thought of what it had felt like to be a bear for even a few moments and smiled.

Picking up the shovel, he growled at Lindie, who wagged her tail, then tugged at his pant legs, the two of them soon headed back to the old house.

35

Bud sat in his sheriff's Land Cruiser with Shorty, watching as a line of cars drove slowly past. He was blocking Main Street for a funeral procession being led by a black pickup with the words *Green River Automotive* painted on the side under what looked like it was supposed to be a whitewall tire, but that actually looked more to Bud like a melting dish of vanilla ice-cream.

This made him think of Howie's, and he wondered if they would have time to drive by there after the funeral and get an ice-cream cone.

"Sure was too bad about old Starbuck, wasn't it?" Shorty asked, nodding toward the line of cars.

"Agreed," Bud said. "And it's sure nice of the town to show up like this. I'm sure Art appreciates it. But I thought it was Breadstick who died."

"Pretty sure it was Starbuck. He was really old."

"Shorty, have you ever heard of a town that has a funeral for a goat?"

"Green River, Utah?" Shorty asked. "I'm curious how Art got so many people to come."

"Well, holding it in Old Man Green's barn was part of the reason."

"Free watermelon spritzer?" Shorty asked.

"Yes, and the hard variety for those with such tastes," Bud replied. "But everyone likes Art, so having a funeral for one of his goats just makes sense."

"They're like his kids. Where will the internment be?"

"Out in the middle of Old Man Green's field, and Art's having a big picnic afterward as a celebration of life. Should be fun."

Shorty said, "I heard there's going to be talk about starting a hockey team."

"No kidding? Is that appropriate at a funeral?" Bud asked.

Shorty laughed. "Where in hellsbells did Art get the idea for hockey? And where's he going to get hockey sticks and things like that?"

"Should be interesting," Bud grinned. "Be glad it's not curling. But Shorty, when this is over, would you mind coming back to my office for a bit? I have to get your advice on something."

"We can talk now, Bud," Shorty replied. "But I don't mind coming over."

"It's about those mittens, and I need to have you look them over. I'm missing something, and I don't know what."

"If you knew, you wouldn't be missing it, right? But did everyone go home from up on the plateau?"

"Yes, Auggie and Maddie went back to Salt Lake, and Cy said he was going back, too, to meet up with Elizabeth. He had Chance with him. He was going to take him to the train station in Helper so he could head to Reno."

As the long line of vehicles tapered off, Bud could see that the last ones were a white SUV and a green pickup. It took a minute, but he finally said, "Shorty! There's the fox hunters!"

"What fox hunters?" Shorty asked. "Man, look at the antennas on those two rigs."

"They were out in Tusher Canyon hunting foxes."

"Bad place to look for foxes," Shorty replied. "But let's get on over to your office.

They were soon there, Bud taking the mittens from the safe and placing them on the desk in front of Shorty.

"Very pretty," Shorty said. "But I think they're too small for me."

"Look at them carefully," Bud advised. "I had a dream where I was told that if I was going to expose secrets, I should at least expose them in their entirety."

"Who told you that?"

"A bear."

"For some reason, that doesn't surprise me," Shorty said.

"Howie and I found Morse code embedded in the lightning bolts. If you rub your fingers across them, you can feel the irregularities. Someone used embroidery to create the dots and dashes of a message."

"Sounds intriguing," Shorty replied, running his fingers across the mittens. "Clever."

Explaining more about the mittens and where they'd come from, Bud added, "My dream implies the mittens hold more secrets, possibly another message. First of all, how would I know another message existed? How could I dream about it and yet not be aware of it? And second, what exactly is the message?"

Examining the gloves more closely, Shorty said, "Your subconscious picked up on something, and the dream's trying to bring it to your awareness. When I look at the knitting, I see a beautiful job, but with lots of irregularities. Your subconscious picked up on these irregularities just as I'm doing, pretty simple. You can't feel them when you run your fingers across them because they're part of the knit and purl process."

"What do you mean, part of the process?" Bud asked.

"My mom was a knitter. Dad always called her a knit-wit, but it was just a joke. Lots of women of her generation were knitters. I don't know much about it, but I do know there are two basic stitches, the knit and the purl. These two stitches function like a binary code: on-off, or zero-one. Morse code is also binary, using dits and dahs, or dots and dashes. Knitting is perfect for covert messaging. Knit stitches form V shapes, while purl stitches create horizontal ones.

This is all you need to encode messages. The person who embroidered the message in the zigzags used the same idea."

"But how would one even know when they were seeing code instead of mistakes?" Bud asked, carefully examining the mittens.

Shorty replied, "It's easy to dismiss a variation as a mistake, like you said, and that's why you need experienced knitters to decipher knitted messages. They're familiar with what normal knitting looks like and could pick up on the oddities. I heard this kind of cryptology was done in both world wars."

"Can you make out anything in these mittens?" Bud asked.

"I just told you everything I know about knitting," Shorty replied. "All from my dear mum, and I'm surprised I remember any of it. But this mittens section here looks like a combination of dots and dashes. I don't know Morse code to know what it could mean."

"Howie! We need Howie!" Bud said.

"He's right across the street, making sandwiches," Shorty said. "All his esoteric and trivial knowledge going to waste. And don't look now, but one of those guys you said were fox hunters is coming over here."

36

"Sheriff, Earl Walker," the tall dark-haired man with a ponytail said, holding out his hand. "We met the other day."

Bud stood to shake hands, noting that Earl was now wearing dark-blue pants and a tan shirt with a star-shaped badge that read, *Investigator, Department of Natural Resources, State of Utah.* In addition, a blue and gold patch on his arm read, *Natural Resources, Utah DNR, Law Enforcement.*

When they'd met before, Earl had simply been wearing a tan shirt with no insignia or badge. Bud suspected he'd been doing some incognito investigative work then, maybe even checking out the fox hunters—it would make sense to join their ranks and make them think you were one of them.

"Nice to meet you. Have a seat," Bud said congenially, while hoping he wouldn't stay long, recalling how bristly Earl had been the day before at Howie's.

"Sheriff Shumway, I'll get right down to business. Can you tell me if you've seen or heard anything about a bear up on the Wasatch?"

"Are you bear hunting?" Bud replied. "I thought you were fox hunting." Noting that Shorty was trying to hide a smile, he added, "Or is this an investigation and not a hunt?"

"It's obviously an investigation or I wouldn't be here in uniform," Earl replied, frowning.

"I'm not up on the plateau much," Bud said. "Though I have been more than usual lately. But no, I haven't seen a bear, though I did hear about that sheepherder that was mauled."

"A sheepherder was mauled?" Earl asked.

"I'm surprised you don't know about it. I don't have the details. Sheriff Davis up in Price can tell you more."

Bud, noting that Earl seemed a bit less cocky, decided to add, "Your grandfather was up there. Still may be, as far as I know, but hopefully not around any bears."

"You know my grandfather?"

"Yes, Cy Walker. He's spent a few nights at my house, at my table. At this point, I know him pretty well."

"He's in the States right now?"

"As far as I know. He was last night. Said he was going back to Salt Lake, though."

"To my Cousin Emma's place, I bet. I wish I'd known that. I'd like to see him."

"He's a fine guy," Bud added. "Is that Christian's wife?"

Earl, looking surprised, replied, "Yes. Seems you know the whole family, eh?"

"Not really," Bud replied. "Though I do know your grandmother, Elizabeth. But back to your interrogation, er, investigation. I really don't know much about bears on the plateau, and I hope your fox hunt's going well."

"It's been a lot of fun," Earl replied, smiling. "I've been able to mix it with work, but the hunt's ending soon. It's National Fox-Hunting Month, you know."

"Did you get any foxes?"

"Oh, sure, all the time. You get good at it after awhile."

Not really wanting to hear the details, Bud asked, "Do you mind if I ask why you, a lawman, are looking for a bear? Don't you usually look for people? Did it break the law or something?"

Earl laughed. "No, but the people responsible for it being here did. We want to trap it and take it back where it came from."

"Where exactly is that?"

"West Yellowstone. It came from a bear rehab place there. Actually, it came from Kodiak Island—it's a Kodiak bear. It was young, and someone found it injured and the rehab place at Yellowstone was the only one that could take it. I'd actually like to see it, but from the viewpoint of outside a trap—me being the one outside the trap, not the bear"

"How did it get on the plateau?" Bud asked.

"We're not sure, but it was kidnapped from the rehab place. It was an inside job."

"Kind of like that art heist at the Montreal Museum, eh? That had to be an inside job, too."

"I'm not familiar with that," Earl said, looking puzzled. "We have no idea why the bear was taken, but we're pretty sure it's the same one we've had reports of here on the plateau, basically because of its size and the fact that it was young and had a white natal-ring collar. I usually deal with poachers, so this is different for me. We're going to try to trap it if we can figure out where it is."

"And you're all on your own out there looking for a big Kodiak bear?" Bud asked. "Those guys get huge."

Looking serious, Earl said, "Yes, and it's not for the faint of heart to be out in the wilds alone, protecting and standing up for the resources of Utah. You know, just one single outdoor resources officer like me is tasked with protecting wildlife, lands, trails, and other resources across an average of 385,000 square acres of the state."

Bud shook his head, then asked, "Is Christian involved?"

Earl, looking surprised, replied, "Somewhat. He works for the Forest Service, but they also deal with wildlife. I know he was up on the plateau. I haven't talked to him today, but he's supposedly getting a trap."

"Was he part of the fox hunt?"

Earl smiled. "He was." He paused, then added, "You know, he had someone with him that day we were in Tusher Canyon, and I bet anything it was Gramps. I didn't know he was down here."

"Were you guys avoiding each other or something?"

"Yes, that's part of the hunt, you know. The fox will always hide until you can actually nail him."

"Sounds kind of brutal," Bud replied.

"Why would you say that?"

"Well, one can't help but feel bad for the fox."

"It's just how it is. You *find* the fox, you *become* the fox," Earl said. "See, you can fox hunt anywhere you want—in towns and cities, in the country, anywhere, but you have to find the fox."

Bud asked, "Hows about Antarctica?"

"Sure, as long as you have a fox. You can always bring one with you, no matter where you are."

"Bring it with you?" Bud asked incredulously. "Bring it with you and then shoot it?"

"You don't shoot it, Sheriff," Earl replied, puzzled. "You hunt it. But I need to go. If you don't mind, would you let me know if you hear anything about this bear?"

"Will do," Bud replied. "But my advice is to look around Joe's Valley."

"Why there specifically?"

"It's just a good place for bears. The dire bears seemed to like it."

"Excuse me? Dire bears?"

"There's been a couple of dire-bear skeletons found near there. Just thinking out loud, but I do suspect that's where you'll find it. Have a big trap, because that fellow's big."

"Have you seen it? I thought you didn't know anything about it."

Like Earl, Bud knew he was sworn to uphold the law, and kidnapping a bear had to be illegal, though he wasn't familiar with exactly what section of the book covered it. But should he mention Maddie and Auggie?

They were definitely involved in all this—but wait, hadn't they said Earl was the one interrogating them before Maddie fled? Earl must suspect something, or he wouldn't have been at the Orange

Olsen house. Bud still suspected it was Maddie who tore the place up and tried to make it look like a bear had done it.

Finally, Bud said, "I haven't seen the bear, but I heard it has a radio collar, so that may help if you can find the frequency it's on."

"How would I know the frequency?" Earl asked somewhat suspiciously. "And how do *you* know that?"

"Look, Earl," Bud said reluctantly. "You talked to the two paleontologists who were excavating a dire-bear skeleton near Joe's Valley. The little bit of info I have, I got from them, and one may be involved in all this. They both work at the U. of U., so you can get ahold of them through the university, but I suspect you already know them— Maddie and Auggie—and you know what, I never did get their last names, but I bet they're probably in the geology department."

Earl, looking surprised, said, "For not knowing anything, you sure know a lot."

Just then, Howie walked in the door, nodding to everyone, then sitting next to Shorty, who was still silently listening.

Bud was now also silent, not sure what else to add, finally deciding he'd said enough.

Howie, noticing everyone was quiet, said, "There's too much QRM in here."

Earl laughed, stood, thanked Bud as he handed him his card, then left.

37

"What's QRM?" Bud asked, watching Earl get into a white pickup with antennas on top.

"Ham talk for static," Howie replied. "Earl got it. He must be a ham."

"His whole family is, so it would make sense," Bud replied.

"He probably goes around saying CQ all the time," Howie said.

"What's that again?" Shorty asked.

Howie replied, "CQ is what you say when you're on the high frequencies and want to talk to someone. You say, *CQ, CQ, anybody home*? It's kind of like asking if there's anybody out there, though I know that's not what it stands for literally. I wrote a song about it. I'd play it for you, but I need my guitar to do it justice."

"Just sing the words," Bud said.

Howie began:

> I was feeling awful lonely,
> Cause my baby left me blue.
> She took my car and radio,
> With nary a CQ.
> So I walked myself to Eddie's Place,

And had a beer or two.
And this song came on the jukebox,
CQ, you fool, CQ.

He added, "It has some more verses, but here's the chorus."

I got the CQ blues,
Just cryin' in my shoes.
No radio, blown fuse,
Just the CQ blues.

Stopping, he said, "This song feels like something I've done before, not at all original."

Shorty replied, "That's because everything that rhymes with blues —shoes, fuse, fools—every song ever written about the blues uses these words, pretty much, anyway."

"Fuse?" Bud asked. "Try using some new words."

Howie asked, "Like queues, cruise, and confused?"

"That should do it," Shorty said.

Howie continued.

So I walked myself to Eddie's Place,
Got in the craft beer queue.
This gal came up and asked me,
Would you like to take a cruise?
CQ, you bet, CQ, I said,
But she just looked confused.

Bud laughed. "I think I like that better."

Shorty added, "Me, too, but you forgot the word blues."

"I'll work more on it later," Howie replied. "I don't have much time. I have to get back to the drive-in, but I came here to ask you guys a question."

"Shoot," Bud said.

"Well, I bought a new HT, and now I'm wondering if I should get some vanity plates. Utah has these cool plates that say *Amateur Radio* on them next to a radio tower, along with your call sign."

"What's not to like?" Shorty asked.

"Well," Howie replied, "You're kind of identifying yourself when you have them. You lose your anonymity."

"Especially if you change your name to your call sign, right?" Shorty asked.

"I guess," Howie replied. "Maybe I won't change it."

"You'd have to be careful to not cut people off or drive too fast," Bud said. "Because everyone would know who you are. But then again, most people wouldn't recognize a call sign, except for other hams, and they would probably be more forgiving, since you're one of them."

Howie sighed. "Maybe I won't get them."

"No," Shorty said. "You earned them. Go ahead and get them. But if you're going back to work, I'm coming over for a sandwich. You coming, Bud?"

"No, I need to make a call," Bud replied. "But Howie, can I borrow your knowledge of Morse code for a few minutes?"

"Sure."

Bud got the mittens from the safe and put them in front of Howie, saying, "I'm just wondering if you see any irregularities in the knitting here that could possibly be Morse code. Shorty and I were talking, and he said sometimes you can make the stitches, the knits and purls, into code. Do you see anything?"

"I thought we already figured all that out," Howie replied.

"I think that may only be part of it. Take a look and see what you think."

Howie studied the mittens, turning them over and over, then finally said, "I can make out some code here. It's kind of sketchy, but I'm sure I see something."

"Tell me what it is, and I'll write it down," Bud said.

Howie replied, "Get Osla home."

"Are you sure?"

"Yes, this one has the full words, no chance to misinterpret it."

"What in the heck could it mean?" Shorty asked. "Are you sure it isn't *ursa* or *oso*, Latin and Spanish for bear? Osla doesn't mean anything."

"I don't know," Howie said. "It's definitely osla. Put it on the 'Figure it Out' list with those coordinates you found. But let's go before the lunch crowd hits, even though Green River doesn't actually have one."

Bud watched as Howie and Shorty crossed the street, wondering what the message could mean.

He soon dialed a Canadian number.

A woman answered.

"Swift Current Museum. Can I help you?"

"I'm Sheriff Bud Shumway calling from Green River, Utah in the U.S. Is there anyone there I can talk to regarding a possible stolen item?"

"You can talk to me. I'm the director."

"I'm calling regarding a pair of mittens that were supposedly stolen from the museum. Are you familiar with this at all?"

"Mr. Shumway, can we do a video call so I can check your ID and see some proof of who I'm talking to?"

Bud replied, "Sure, if I can figure out how to do it."

"Don't you have a smart phone?"

"*It* may be smart, but *I'm* not when it comes to operating it."

Bud could hear her sigh, then say, "All right, tell me more about this stolen pair of mittens."

"It's a pair of mittens knit during WWII by Queen Elizabeth, though she was still a princess at that time."

"We had some British mittens. Are they purple with yellow streaks?"

"Yes. Were they stolen?"

"Not that I'm aware of. They belong to one of our residents, Elizabeth Walker. We had them on loan. Her husband, Cy, is one of our elders. He said she wanted them back, so we released them to him. He signed for them, and that was the end of that. I hope they bring them back some day. They were beautiful. Does that answer your question?"

"Yes, it certainly does. Thank you for your time."

"You're most welcome," she said. "And if you're ever in this area, come visit us. We have a nice museum here, even though it's small."

Bud was ready to hang up, but then remembered something else. "Say, are you familiar with Wanuskewin?"

"Oh, sure," she replied. "The heritage park? It's nearby. There's a lot of early history there. I go there quite often. I like to hear the sound of the thundering bison."

"Just like in the old days, eh?" Bud asked. "Do you ever hear the sounds of the old rituals? You know, people chanting and drumming, that kind of thing."

After a pause, she replied, "No, that would be kind of weird."

"But you said you hear the bison," Bud replied.

"There's a herd of bison there," she answered. "You can hear them when they run around. Have a nice day, Mr. Shumway."

Feeling kind of sheepish, Bud hung up, wondering what other things he was misinterpreting.

He stood, looking out the window, where he could see that Shorty was now sitting at a table at Howie's, talking to someone.

Since there wasn't anything much going on, Bud decided he might as well join him. He put on his jacket, locked the office door, and walked across the street, just to recognize who Shorty was talking to—it was Chance! When had he come back?

Bud heard him say, "Shorty, here on Earth, stupid stuff happens for no good reason all the time. Maybe it's been awhile since your last visit?"

Shorty laughed, then said, "So that's how you explain getting on a train going the opposite direction from where you wanted to go? You just say that stupid stuff happens all the time?"

"It's true," Chance replied.

"And you had nothing to do with it?" Shorty asked.

"I was on automatic pilot."

"Or maybe you just missed being in Green River," Bud said,

sitting by Shorty. "But fellas, I have a question for you. What does it mean when someone says, 'You *find* the fox, you *become* the fox?'"

"It's deep philosophy," Chance said. "Don't try to understand things like that. It messes with your brain and makes you unhappy, because there's no answer. Before you know it, you're all tangled up in things like yoga poses and deep breathing and you want to go to Tibet and become a monk. Don't even get started."

Bud laughed. "Say, Chance, I assume Cy gave you a ride to Helper, where you got on the train. Did he go on up to Salt Lake?"

"No. He said he was going back up to Joe's Valley. I told him to watch out for that big bear up there, and he just laughed. He said he finally knew where one of the Grandfathers was, whatever that means."

"It looks like we might be in for another search and rescue," Shorty said as Bud sighed, wondering who had told Cy about the petroglyph in the cave, though he was pretty sure he knew.

It had to have been Maddie.

38

Bud sat on the back patio of the bungalow, playing his harmonica as the dogs slept at his feet. He'd just talked to Kale, who would be leaving soon with Molly on vacation, the harvest now complete.

Bud wished them well, wondering if Ireland was really as green as people said, thinking he should learn how to play *Danny Boy*, though maybe that was an English tune. He tried it for a moment, then, deciding it was too hard, went back to *Summertime*, then finally, *Red River Valley*, as it was really one of the few songs he could play while trying to think, since he knew it so well.

As he played, he thought about when he'd first met Christian and Cy in the Melon Rind Cafe, and how interested Cy had been in his petroglyph photo from Tusher Canyon.

He'd been pleasantly surprised earlier when Wilma Jean had told him someone had just bought it, though she didn't know who, as Maureen had been working. It was the first photo Bud had ever sold, and he was pretty sure it would be his last, unless he bought one from himself.

Wondering if he could write buying his own stuff off on his taxes, maybe itemized as some kind of therapy, he began thinking about the mittens in his safe. Maybe it was time to get them out and give them back to Cy or Elizabeth, assuming he ever saw either of them again, though he had a hunch he would be seeing Cy, and maybe not before long.

The coded message about Bletchley Park made sense, but the one about Osla seemed odd. What in the world could *Get Osla home* mean? Was Osla a person? If so, it was the first time he'd ever heard the name.

He went inside and got his laptop, bringing it to the back deck. He keyed in *Osla*. He couldn't find much about it, other than it was a Scottish woman's name from the Shetland Islands.

He tried again, this time keying in *Osla woman's name*. A lengthy article came up about a woman named Osla Benning.

Osla Benning was a Canadian debutante who ended up in England after her parents divorced. Lord Mountbatten was her godfather, and he introduced Osla to his nephew, Prince Phillip, who was in the British Navy. Mountbatten was the admiral of the fleet Phillip served on and was a close relative of the British royal family. Osla was working as a codebreaker at Bletchley Park.

Osla and Phillip fell in love and dated. She was described as a beautiful woman with dark hair, alabaster white skin, a great sense of humor, and a gentle loving nature.

Things got complicated when Phillip met Princess Elizabeth. Her family life was very attractive to him, as he'd grown up basically in chaos, and he began going to visit her family frequently. Princess Elizabeth fell madly in love with Philip, and they eventually married, though much later.

Osla ended up marrying a baron. She told her daughter that she'd been in love with a navy officer, and she had a brooch he gave her, but she never revealed who he was. Later, the truth came out through photos and other witnesses.

Bud leaned back. It was another Bletchley Park connection, and it appeared that Osla and the person the mittens were made for, Elizabeth Walker's grandmother, must have known each other, as well as knowing Princess Elizabeth.

Was Princess Elizabeth jealous of Osla, but being a royal, as well as being young, was unable to voice her frustration, so instead had surreptitiously asked her Canadian cousin to help get Osla back to Canada by using Morse code to send the message, *Get Osla home*?

He now thought back to all the fox-hunting activity and the conversation with Earl. What had he meant by *You find the fox, you become the fox*? And what was going to happen at the MK Tunnels? As sheriff, it was in his county, and he figured he probably should go check it out, though he wasn't wanting to see a bunch of poor dead foxes.

He was surprised at the enthusiasm Earl had displayed for the whole thing, but such was the way of hunters. It was a good thing Molly wouldn't be attending the celebration, as he knew she would chew them all out.

He began nodding off, even though the sun was still high in the afternoon sky. Wilma Jean wouldn't be off work for several more hours, and he decided he should stay awake in case she brought some leftovers, besides, something was bothering him, tugging at his sense of responsibility, though he couldn't quite place what it was.

He startled as his phone rang, hoping it wasn't a call regarding some shenanigan he'd have to go take care of, like the time a guy called and said someone had come into his home and winterized his pipes when he was out of town, or the time old Orrin Coleman had called at midnight "just wanting to chat."

"Yell-ow," Bud answered.

It was Howie.

"Sheriff, Chance and I are making tomorrow's work plans, and we need to know what you want painted on your office door for Melon Days."

Bud laughed. "Hows about a melon?"

"We could paint a big dire bear eating a melon," he could hear Chance say in the background.

Bud sat up straight, realizing what had been tugging at his subconscious.

"Howie, I need to get over to the Dire Bear Cafe ASAP. I completely forgot what Chance said about Cy going over there. I have a feeling he's going to get himself into trouble."

"Geez Louise, Sheriff," Howie replied. "You're right. But you shouldn't go alone. I'll go with you. Come down to the drive-in, and I'll have us some sandwiches and drinks ready."

"OK, Howie, and thanks," Bud replied. "But I have a hunch we may be out awhile. I'm going to leave Lindie home in case we do run into that bear. You may want to tell Maureen there's a possibility you'll be gone overnight."

"You think so, Sheriff?"

"It's possible. The plateau's a big place, and Cy could be out wandering anywhere. He's proven himself on that one."

Bud could hear Chance say, "Ask him if I can come."

Bud replied, "Chance is welcome, but tell him to bring a warm coat in case we end up staying out, and tell him he may be getting up close and personal with some of that wildlife he paints on the train cars. As long as he's good with that, he's welcome. The more the merrier if we need to start searching. I'm going to call Earl and let him know."

"Sounds good," Howie replied.

"And don't forget your radio, Howie, as well as the FPV goggles for the radio collar. You still have those, don't you?"

"I do. I'll have to run home to get them."

"They may come in handy," Bud said, not realizing how accurate his prediction would become.

39

Bud and Howie and Chance stood, silent, hidden behind a rock just up the hill from the Dire Bear Cafe, Howie holding the FPV goggles to his eyes. As Bud started to say something, Howie held up his hand, then whispered, "Sheriff, listen to this, but be real quiet. The audio's on, and it goes both ways."

Though Bud could barely make out anything through the goggles, which Howie held a bit tipped so they could all look, he thought he could see what looked like a man standing in front of a large rock, and he knew it was Cy and the petroglyph, or Grandfather. The camera seemed to tower over everything, and though Bud could barely make out what Cy was saying, it sounded like, "Who's in here?"

Howie held his finger to his lips, motioning Bud to be quiet, as the man continued. "There's someone in here. Who is it?"

Now Bud could make out a second voice, though he couldn't see who it was.

"It's me, Cy. You know who it is."

"Maddie? Why are you here?"

She replied, "I knew you'd come when I told you about the Grandfather. I need to talk to you."

"Why here?"

"I think they're catching on, Cy, and I needed to talk to you some place where they wouldn't be watching, to ask you to keep your promise to not say anything. No one can hear us here."

Howie looked intently at Bud, then started to whisper something, but Bud put his fingers to his lips.

"Who are you talking about?" Cy asked. "I thought you went home. Is there really a Grandfather here, or did you trick me into coming back?"

"I did go home, but now I'm back. Why would I trick you?"

"Maybe you're hoping the bear will get me. Where is the Grandfather?"

Bud and Howie and Chance stood waiting as the figures passed from view and all was quiet. Bud figured they were now examining the large rock with the rib carving.

Howie again tried to whisper something to Bud, who shook his head as if to say, *not now*.

Partially back in view, Maddie said, "See, I knew it was a ribstone, what you call a Grandfather. It's an incredible discovery, but Cy, you have to promise not to say anything about the bear. Remember your promise when we started all this."

"I had no idea what the bear would do," Cy replied. "And I had no idea you would slam Christian and break into his pickup. What were you hoping to find?"

Now Howie was urgently tugging at Bud's sleeve, trying to whisper something in his ear.

Maddie replied, "I was mad, but I didn't mean to hurt him. I thought he'd taken my goggles. I regretted doing that, as I found them later at the house."

Chance pulled on Bud's arm and whispered, "Sheriff, you do realize we're looking through the FPV goggles. Howie's trying to tell you that those goggles are transmitting the view from the radio collar..."

Howie had a panicked look on his face.

Bud finished the sentence, "...which is *on* the bear! That bear's in the cave with them, but they don't know it! Howie, say something!"

"I don't want to startle it," Howie whispered. "It might make it attack."

Just then, Howie's radio, which was in a holster on his belt, broke into a loud squelch as someone kerchunked the nearby Ford Ridge repeater. This was followed by the repeater signaling its Morse code identification, loud and clear.

Howie cried out in dismay, "Son of a rabid ferret!"

Bud could see Maddie and Cy both startle and begin slowly backing up.

"Play some Metallica, Maddie," Howie yelled through the goggles. Turning to Bud, he added, "Sheriff, we need to get up there."

Bud could see that the camera was getting closer and closer to Maddie and Cy, and he knew the bear was approaching them. And as the camera began swaying back and forth, he knew the bear was ready to charge.

"Good bear," Howie yelled into the goggles. "Pacifistic, quiet, gentle bear! Bud, this is just like my dream, except there's no hunter..."

As Howie said it, Bud could see a flash reflect off Cy's silver belt buckle, followed by a loud reverberating sound. There was a pause, the camera tumbled to the ground, and he knew someone had shot the bear.

Howie turned to Bud and said, "Sheriff, if this were in a book, isn't this where the editor would add a note telling the reader to suspend disbelief?"

Bud nodded his head, saying, "Probably."

He and Howie and Chance were soon at the cave, just in time to see two men standing in the entrance, both holding rifles. Maddie and Cy were outside, obviously shaken and disoriented. The still form of a large bear lay on the cave floor in a heap, looking to Bud kind of like a bear rug in one of those ritzy magazines about fancy cabins in places like Jackson or Aspen.

"Sheriff Shumway?" Maddie asked. "What are you doing here?"

"Just a little bear hunt, Maddie," Bud replied. "One using tranquilizer darts."

"It's my grandbabies, Christian and Earl!" Cy exclaimed.

Christian stood by Cy, saying, "Gramps, we don't have a lot of time until this bear wakes up. You and Maddie and the sheriff's friends need to go on down to that house and hole up until we come down."

Earl, now standing over the bear, said, "Christian, I think we're going to need all hands on deck to get this bear down to the culvert trap in your truck. We don't have a lot of time, folks. I gave him a big dose of tranq, but he's huge, so it won't last long. Heave ho."

Bud wasn't sure how, but they managed to eventually half-drag half-carry the bear down the hill and get it into the big trap, which was basically a culvert with a large door welded onto it, with a small hoist attached to the truck bed.

"Where will you take it?" Maddie asked, covered with bear fur and dirt.

Christian replied, "Back to the refuge in West Yellowstone, but first to a place up by Helper that does wildlife rehab, where they'll check it over and get it ready for the trip. Is that your radio collar?"

Maddie hesitated until Cy said, "You might as well tell them."

"Yes. It's mine," she replied.

"We're going to be wanting to talk to you some more about all this," Earl said. "Right now, we need to get this bear taken care of, but you can count on a visit in the near future."

"Are you going to arrest me?" Maddie asked.

"You'll definitely be held accountable," Earl continued. "There will be fines, I'm sure, but it will depend on the judge as to what else is implemented. I know where you work, so we'll be paying you a visit. Go on home. We need to get going before this bear wakes up."

"Cy was involved," Maddie said. "He drove the truck."

"Is that true, Gramps?" Christian asked with concern.

"Guilty as charged," Cy replied. "But I was just doing what the Queen told me to do, like any good subject."

"You mean Maddie?" Howie asked.

"No, the Queen—Queen Elizabeth the Second. The *real* Queen. The one across the Pond. I can prove it."

"The Queen passed away some time ago, Gramps, but we'll catch up with you back in Price," Christian said. "This isn't your first rodeo. Maybe there's a reason both of your grandsons are in law enforcement. But Grandmum's on her way to meet you there, and Earl and I will also be visiting with you, as soon as we get this bear back. Sheriff Shumway's offered his house for us to reconnoiter."

"I can't wait," Cy said as Earl and Christian got into the truck. "It'll be nice catching up on things with you rascally kids. And take good care of that bear. It wasn't easy getting it down here, you know."

They watched as the pair drove off, the culvert trap barely bouncing behind them, the weight of the bear holding it down.

Howie handed Maddie the goggles, saying, "I guess we won't need these any more."

Just then, a voice came on his radio, saying, "AFØXN, this is KFØSTL. The fox hunt's over. Hope to see you at the tunnels tomorrow. KFØSTL, clear."

"Roger that. I'll be there. AFØXN, over," a voice said, and Bud knew it was Earl.

Somehow, he knew he and Howie needed to be at the tunnels, too, to make sense of everything. But first, he had a meeting to attend —in his own living room in the house in Price.

40

"He just doesn't look like a common criminal, does he?" Elizabeth asked.

"That's because I'm not common," Cy replied. "I'm one of a kind."

Cy looked at Earl and Christian, who sat across from him on patio chairs. Bud had offered the house in Price for them all to meet and decompress, and he'd already called Wilma Jean to tell her they wouldn't be coming home until the next day—he wanted to go to the celebration at the MK Tunnels.

Cy asked, "Am I going to be arrested?"

"Yes," Christian replied. "We haven't done it yet because we can't decide which one of us gets the honors. Getting that bear into that trap then back out again at the Helper rehab was something that someone deserves being arrested over."

"You're sure a good role model for your kids," Elizabeth said to Cy.

"My kids turned out fine," Cy replied. "It's the grandkids I worry about."

Elizabeth said to Bud, "Christian's going to take him home next week, assuming Canada will take him back."

"I'm perfectly legal," Cy replied. "I have my driver's license."

"Look, Gramps," Christian said. "Earl and I both talked with our supervisors, and neither feel there's enough grounds for an arrest. But we all agree you need to go home before you get yourself in serious trouble. But before you do, could you tell us how it came about that you partnered with someone who talked you into driving a Kodiak bear into Utah?"

"She was just following the Queen's orders, like I was," Cy replied.

"Go ahead and tell them where you got these supposed orders," Elizabeth commanded.

"They're right there in those mittens," Cy replied.

Bud asked, "You're aware of the Morse code messages in the mittens?"

Cy grimaced, saying, "We're hams, we can read code. Don't you think we already deciphered the mittens?"

Bud was surprised. He asked, "What does *Get Osla home* mean?"

"That's the message from the Queen I'm referring to," Cy said impatiently. "It's obvious she's talking about the bear. Osla means bear."

Elizabeth laughed. "Ursa means bear, not Osla." She turned to Bud. "Cy is famous for taking things and giving them whatever meaning he wants. He can be very creative."

"Queen Elizabeth, your very own namesake, knitted those mittens, Elizabeth," Cy said. "What else would she be talking about? She's advocating for bears, get them home, which is what I tried to do."

Now laughing, Elizabeth said, "Just tell us the rest of the story."

Cy, looking a bit miffed, said, "OK. I met Maddie in the Swift Current Museum. She was researching bears, and with her being a paleontologist, we both liked old stuff, so we got to talking. She told me she knew of a place in Utah with at least one Grandfather, though she just called it rock art."

"There are literally thousands of rock-art sites in Utah, Gramps," Christian said.

"I know, but she'd gone through the Wanuskewin and knew what the ribstones were. She said she knew of at least one."

"She told me it was a shaft straightener," Bud commented.

"I'm not surprised," Cy replied. "She didn't want anyone but me to know about it. She understood how old it might be, and we were kind of partners in crime."

"Kind of doesn't begin to describe it," Earl said.

"Well, we just had an immediate trust for each other, probably based on our philosophies about old stuff. We got to talking, and I knew she was the one who could show me the Grandfathers, and I could do what the Queen wanted regarding the bear. We could help each other that way."

"Give it up, Gramps," Christian said. "We're not buying the Queen thing. You just wanted to see the rock art and agreed to whatever she said."

"Whatever. Anyway, she picked me up at the old border crossing near Glacier National Park, the one near Polebridge that they shut down. I then repaid the favor by helping her with the bear. She already had made arrangements for getting it, I just helped drive it down here."

"In a rented U-Haul?" Earl asked.

"Yes. Some guy from the rehab place helped. She paid him. We had to drive fast because the bear was tranquillized, and you know how that goes." He nodded to Earl.

"That's who we'll probably be arresting next," Earl said. "Or at least the wildlife guys in Montana will be."

"Why did she threaten you and Christian up on the plateau when you were stuck?" Bud asked. "There was mud all over the van, so I suspected she'd been up there, either her or Auggie. I knew you were trying to not implicate someone, but I wasn't sure who. I thought maybe it was Earl or even the sheep rancher. And why were you guys up there in the first place? It wasn't on the way to Delta."

Cy continued. "Maddie was mad at Christian. She had asked Christian to help from the get-go, given his expertise, not even knowing we were related. She called his office in Salt Lake, told him about her ideas, and he of course refused, and she was pretty mad about it. He threatened to arrest her. Christian later found out there was a bear on the plateau and wanted to go see if he could spot it, so we drove up there. It was part of his job. What Maddie did was wrong, and I regret making up the story about the bear following us to cover for her, but at the time, it seemed like a good idea. I was surprised she actually slammed Christian, but I guess digging in the dirt builds up your muscles, as well as your ability to get physical. Christian never saw who it was, though I did, but I didn't want to get her in trouble. It was all highly illegal, and now she's in a lot of trouble."

"And you aren't?" Elizabeth asked. "Seems you just didn't want to get yourself in trouble."

"All I did was drive a truck. I had no idea what was in it, and I have a driver's license."

"Which maybe you shouldn't," Earl said. "But Maddie didn't know we were all related?"

"No," Cy replied. "But she's not all bad. She just wanted to see if a bear could survive in a different environment. It was research for cloning a dire bear. Kodiak Island is rainforest."

Bud asked, "Did she tear up the Orange Olsen house, or was it really a bear?"

"She did it. Earl had been interrogating her, and she knew her time was about up. She wanted to run away but didn't want it to look like she left because she was in trouble."

"I noticed she didn't tear up anything important, like their books," Bud said.

"Exactly," Cy replied. "And Auggie's a good guy. He had no part in any of this. He's going to make sure the Grandfather in the cave is taken care of. It's big science, a big find."

He then turned to Elizabeth. "If Osla isn't a bear, what is it?"

"It's a woman's name," Bud answered. "I have a theory about what was going on, but it basically was a request from Princess Elizabeth to get rid of a competitor named Osla. But since you already read the code in the mittens, I presume you know about the message in the yellow lightning bolts?"

"Yes," Elizabeth replied. "The family always suspected that our grandmother was at Bletchley Park from a few things she said, but she was bound by the British Secrecy Act and couldn't elaborate. As you know, Princess Elizabeth became Queen Elizabeth II. She was a well-known knitter. Rumor has it that she sent gifts to all the women who had been part of the war effort at Bletchley Park, but no one could ever discuss them or acknowledge them. My grandmother said she received something, but she couldn't talk about it, but now we know it was the mittens with messages in Morse code. Later, she also received a substantial honorarium, which she used to purchase part of the land that the Wanuskewin Heritage Park is on, which she later donated. Anyway, she was an electronics expert. She had a ham radio license and is the reason the rest of the family is into it."

"What a nice family tradition," Howie said, handing Christian the radio Bud had found in Tusher Canyon. "Bud found this. It was nice having it for awhile, but I got myself one now. You can keep the extra battery banks."

"That's fantastic! I wondered where it went. What did you get?" Christian asked.

"Another Yaesu just like yours. They're classics."

"And this also belongs to your family," Bud said, handing Elizabeth the mittens. "But I'm still wondering why Christian left the radio and mittens out in Tusher Canyon."

Christian replied, "I really had no idea the mittens were Grandmum's and were of importance. Gramps sometimes has some pretty eclectic stuff around, and I figured they'd make good protection for the radio, which I left with the PTT button set to *on* so it would transmit, as it was the fox. I had a work call come in, and the reception was so poor that Gramps and I went out of the canyon so I could take it. When we came back, everything was gone, and none of the fox hunters had it. I was kind of mystified, to be honest, since it's such a remote place."

Bud asked, "Are you going back to Salt Lake now?"

"Grams and Gramps are," Christian said. "We were supposed to be going to Delta, Colorado for the powwow, but we obviously got sidetracked, plus my outfit got ruined."

"Delta, Colorado?" Bud asked with surprise. "Not Delta, Utah?"

Christian replied, "Colorado. The Utes have a big powwow over there every year. But tomorrow, Earl and I are going to the fox-hunt celebration. You guys are invited. It's great fun, lots of touting of our many successful hunts, and all the foxes will be there."

"We plan to do that," Bud said. "You have the foxes on display?"

Christian looked puzzled. "I don't know that I would describe it exactly as being on display, but they'll be there. There's a KrakenSDR as a prize for the best hunt."

"I think Bud deserves that." Chance now spoke for the first time. "He keeps finding your grandpa on the plateau, kind of over and over and over, like that movie *Groundhog Day*."

Cy turned to Elizabeth. "So this means you're not going to divorce me?"

Christian replied, "Gramps, if you had a dollar for every time Grams threatened to divorce you, you'd be able to buy her a nice pickup."

Everyone soon left, except for Bud and Howie and Chance, who would spend the night there and head out the next morning for the MK Tunnels, though Bud wasn't keen on the sight of the bounty from the fox hunts.

He missed his wife and the dogs, especially Lindie, and would much prefer to be in the Big Empty, wondering if he should wander around aimlessly.

Instead, he ended up playing a game of checkers with Chance.

41

"There were Americans at Bletchley Park, too," Howie said as he, Bud, and Chance bounced along the dirt road that had brought them from Price to the Swell, in search of the MK tunnels.

Howie continued. "We played a big role in deciphering enemy messages, and of course, we had our own American heroes—the Navajo code talkers. And the U.S. was the only country that developed a totally unbreakable code machine. It was called SIGABA and was the most secure cryptographic machine used by any nation in WWII."

"What does SIGABA mean?" Chance asked.

Howie replied, "As far as I know, it's not an acronym and doesn't stand for anything. It's just a code word."

"Fellas, we're now on the Green River cutoff, almost to the turnoff to the Buckhorn Wash road," Bud said. "We're going to work our way on old roads east of the wash itself, then drop down a bit to the tunnels. We'll come back and rejoin the cutoff and take it home when we're done."

"Good thing we have those coordinates or we'd get lost, right Sheriff?" Howie asked.

Bud groaned. "I forgot them. But I think I know where to go

anyway. If we don't find the tunnels, we'll have a picnic and go on home. I'm not real crazy about this fox-hunting thing, anyway."

They had now caught up to a couple of other vehicles.

"We can follow those guys," Chance said. "They look like they know where they're going."

"And they have antennas on top," Howie added.

They soon took a rough side road, and after a couple of miles winding through some desert flats, took yet another turn, all the time following the other two vehicles.

After several more turns, Chance asked, "Are you sure you can find your way back, Mr. Shumway? Lots of twists and turns."

"We know what we're doing," Howie grinned. "We've been lost out here before. But we can just follow everyone back."

"What if they're lost, too?" Chance asked. "What's going to happen out here, anyway? What are these tunnels?"

Howie replied, "The MK Tunnels are several tunnels blasted into the hillsides by the Department of Defense to see how the rock would react to missile attacks. The sandstone didn't withstand the attacks very well, so they moved on over to the Colorado Springs area where they established NORAD, the North American Aerospace Defense Command."

"Wow," Chance replied. "This could've been a military base."

Howie said, "This is a great place to have a hamfest, since a lot of hams are also history buffs."

"Looks like we've arrived," Bud said, nodding toward a group of vehicles parked near a fenced-off area. As they approached, they could make out people milling around several large portable tables laden with food and drinks. Earl and Christian stood out, as both were wearing colorful Hawaiian shirts.

"Picnic stuff!" Chance said.

Bud parked the Land Cruiser, and they joined the crowd.

"Sheriff Shumway!" Christian called out. "Glad you could make it. We're about ready to start the ceremony. Grab some chow."

It wasn't long before a short stocky man, standing on a nearby rock, began yelling, "Hey, folks, time to get this show on the road.

Welcome to the end of National Fox-Hunting Month. I'm with club KL7ADB out of Wasilla, Alaska and have been asked by your Sinbad Club president to do the honors today."

After waiting for the applause to die down, he continued. "We'll be awarding certificates to the most successful hunters, as well as a KrakenSDR to the grand champ of fox hunting. And congrats to everyone on one of the most successful hunts I've ever had the privilege to be a part of. Never seen so many foxes get pelted, for lack of a better word."

Bud couldn't help but grimace, thinking of Molly and the beautiful red foxes that hung around her back door, waiting for scraps. He was glad she was most likely on her way to Ireland.

"But first, I'd like to give a hat tip to Emery County Sheriff Bud Shumway, who's joined us today. We're going to make him our guest of honor. We always appreciate having the law on our side, especially when it comes to our hunting activities. We've never had a fox get lost, but if we did, it's good to know that people like Sheriff Shumway are out there and ready to join us on the hunt. A round of applause."

Howie grinned, joining in the raucous clapping for Bud, who was wondering how one searched for a lost fox—maybe it was like putting out an APB for a lost bear.

"OK, I'd like for all the foxes to hold up your hands."

More than half the crowd held up their hands as the other half clapped.

Bud was confused. Foxes? Hold up your hands?

"There will be commemorative certificates on the table when we're done, though you'll have to fill in your names. And now, for the big prize, the KrakenSDR. Drum roll, please."

The hams all began drumming on whatever was nearby, which, in most cases, was their legs.

The MC yelled, "And it goes to Christian Walker! Christian found over 35 foxes in a display of amazing technical ability and savvy. Congrats, Christian."

After the clapping stopped, Christian said, "I'd like for the prize to go to someone else, as I used my family's Kraken to find all these foxes. Or maybe we could auction it off for the club."

Everyone clapped again, and the MC continued. "That's very generous of you, Christian. We'll have an auction, and the proceeds will go to the club to help maintain their repeater up on Ford Ridge. OK, do I hear fifty dollars? These rigs start at over $500, folks, and that doesn't include the antennas, which are over $200."

As the bidding started in earnest, Bud turned to Howie. "Where's all the foxes? I sure wasn't looking forward to seeing them."

"You're looking at them, Bud," Howie replied.

"You mean they hunt each other?"

Howie laughed. "No, the foxes are the hams who hide their rigs for others to find, or you could say the foxes are the transmitters. I should've known what they were doing, Bud, but I've always heard it called T-Hunting, for transmitter hunting, and you have to keep in mind that I haven't been around hams for a long time. But it's also called fox hunting. The person serving as the fox hides their transmitter, and others try to locate it using triangulation. Whoever finds it gets to be the fox and hide their rig next. It's a typical ham form of entertainment."

"So, you *find* the fox, you *become* the fox?" Bud asked with a grin. "And all this time, I thought it was real animals, real foxes."

"I still think it holds some kind of existential meaning," Chance said.

"If you don't have a KrakenSDR," Howie explained, "You need a highly directional antenna, a receiver, and a map. You point the antenna toward the signal and record the heading where the signal from the transmitter is the strongest, then go to a new location and do it again. Eventually, you can draw a line along the headings, and where they cross will be where the transmitter is located. There are international competitions called Radiosport all over the world."

"And that's how the FCC caught the people who were talking to you up at Scofield Reservoir, eh?" Bud asked.

"Exactly," Howie replied. "There's a practical use for this fun as well. The hunters can find a source of interference like a malfunctioning piece of electronics or an illegal transmitter. It's especially handy when someone transmits on airplane or public safety frequencies."

Bud shook his head. "And all this time I thought..."

"Hey," Howie said. "The club's headquartered up in Price, but I see a few Green Riverites. I'm going to go say hello. You're not in a hurry, are you?"

"Never in a hurry," Bud replied. "Unless Chance is."

Chance replied, "No, I'm fine. When we're done here, I'm going back to Green River to finish all the window stuff, then do a mural on Howie's new caboose, assuming he can get it down to his place."

"What kind of mural?"

"He wants me to do one of that big steam engine they call Big Boy. It should be fun, and after that, I've decided to start my own mural business. Instead of my art on trains crisscrossing the country, I myself will crisscross the country, leaving my art for people everywhere to admire, enriching and elevating lives. But Sheriff, I have a question for you."

"Shoot."

"Do you think you could teach a dog to bark in Morse code and be able to communicate better with humans?"

Bud laughed. "I'm sure it's possible, but first, you'd have to teach them how to spell, which might take awhile."

"Sounds good. Oh, and I keep forgetting to tell you, but I was in your wife's cafe with Howie the other day, and this Christian guy came in and bought one of your photos, the petroglyph one. He said it was for his grandfather. I thought that was way cool."

Bud was silent for a moment, thinking back to the day when Christian and Cy had first come into the cafe, then replied, "Thanks for telling me. Now let's go have seconds."

They filled up their plates, had a nice picnic, then headed down the road and on to better things.

∾

ABOUT THE AUTHOR

Chinle Miller writes from southeastern Utah and western Colorado, where she spends most of her time wandering with her dogs. She has an A.S. in Geology, a B.A. in Anthropology, and an M.A. in Linguistics. She holds an Amateur Extra ham license.

If you enjoyed this book, you'll also enjoy Bud's look at his little town of Green River, Utah in *A Slice of Life in Watermelon Town,* as well as the other books in the Bud Shumway mystery series starting with the first, *The Ghost Rock Cafe.*

And Chinle has a series of national park books for readers from age 8 on up, the first being *The Tuxedo Cat Kids in the Mystery of the Lost Arch* (set in Arches), with fantastic artwork by Moab native Cary Cox.

And don't miss *Uranium Daughter, Wandering off the Map,* and *The Impossibility of Loneliness,* also by Chinle Miller.

And if you enjoy Bigfoot stories, you'll love *Rusty Wilson's Bigfoot Campfire Stories* and his many other Bigfoot books, as well as his popular *Chasing After Bigfoot: My Search for North America's Most Elusive Creature.*

Cover by Cary Cox

www.ingramcontent.com/pod-product-compliance
Lightning Source LLC
Chambersburg PA
CBHW051646260626
47170CB00004B/1365